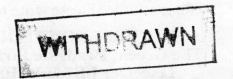

BLACK JO OF THE PECOS

Black Josephine Callard was a mystery. Nobody knew where she came from or whither she returned. The one certainty about her was that she ran a highly successful gang. Deputy U.S. Marshal Frank Haggard at last ran up against her and her confederates near the Pecos river, but everything went wrong when he tried to make his arrests. He would have to exercise all his cunning and ability to stay alive before he could defeat the gang and solve the mystery.

JEFF BLAINE

BLACK JO
OF
THE PECOS

Complete and Unabridged

LINFORD
Leicester

First published in Great Britain in 1995 by
Robert Hale Limited
London

First Linford Edition
published 1997
by arrangement with
Robert Hale Limited
London

British Library CIP Data

Blaine, Jeff, *1928 –*
Black Jo of the Pecos.—Large print ed.—
Linford western library
1. English fiction—20th century
2. Large type books
I. Title
823.914 [F]

ISBN 0-7089-5000-0

Published by
F. A. Thorpe (Publishing) Ltd.
Anstey, Leicestershire
Set by Words & Graphics Ltd.
Anstey, Leicestershire
Printed and bound in Great Britain by
T. J. Press (Padstow) Ltd., Padstow, Cornwall

This book is printed on acid-free paper

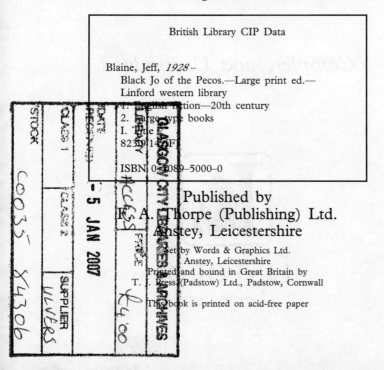

1

IT was here all right. Improbable
as it had seemed at the time, that
hunter down in Clarion Town had
told him the truth.

Deputy U.S. Marshal Frank Haggard
gazed around the granite mouth of the
tunnel which he had just entered. It
was a cheerless hole, unnaturally still
yet softly echoing, and a draught
stole lightly through it, cold as death
itself. Glancing back over his shoulder,
Haggard gazed into the rock-filled
shadows of the long-since dried-up
watercourse by which he had approached
this place from the main flow of the
Pecos river, and something inside him
shrank from the jagged ridges and
towering walls of grey rock that
he could see stooping at him on
either hand. The harsh scene and
its grim atmosphere seemed to warn

at least and even to promise trouble ahead. Pulling himself together sharply, Haggard thumbed back his hammer on the cartridge in the breech of his Winchester rifle. Well, if it had to be, it had to be. He was ready for it. For if, as the hunter had also assured him, the tunnel amounted to an emergency exit from Black Josephine Callard's hideout at the front of this rock mass which he was about to penetrate, he would soon be challenging a bevy of fast guns — since the men of Black Jo's band were all hand-picked villains of the bloodiest skills and reputations — but he would only become certain of what he had to face when he reached the end of this tunnel, or its beginning, depending on how you looked at it.

Haggard moved slowly forward, heading into the dark; and it was dark, too, almost impenetrably so even at this stage; but he dared not carry a light, since that would certainly betray his presence to anybody in the cave at the further end of this passage long before he could get the drop on them. Not that the darkness should worry him much, of course, for he had likewise been promised that the tunnel was of no great length and perfectly safe to walk through without a light. So, ignoring the claustrophobic presence of the untold millions of tons of granite pressing in upon him, he groped his way into the stygian folds of the way ahead, telling himself every other moment that he would shortly be seeing the glow of the sun before him again. After all, disregarding its obvious drawbacks, this walk in the dark was the wisest way of starting this attempt to capture the Callard gang, because Black Jo — as the Southwest called the Callard girl — could have no idea that the secret of the emergency way out of her hideout was known to anybody other than herself and the members of her robber band. He had never dreamed of such a feature himself until he had been told about it. Indeed, the location of Black Jo's hideout itself had been an unsolved mystery to him until that hunter from the Pecos country had provided the clue.

An echo trembled, its vibrations rippling in either direction along the passage, and the unseen roof above Frank Haggard gave a faint, tearing crack. Dust and tiny bits of rock came slurring down, the fragments peppering the deputy marshal's head and shoulders with small impacts and the dust stopping his nose a little and drying his mouth. He halted, sweating coldly, and shook himself, scared as he had seldom been scared before — and his heart hammered and chills ran up and down his spine, while his imagination filled with visions of being buried alive and the voice of his mind shrieked at him to scamper back to the spot from which he had started. But there was no future in flight, and he took another hold on his shaking body; then, with teeth firmly clenched, went forward, the dry precipitation from above having ceased and the roof resumed its silence.

All at once the rock up there again split softly, and some more dust and minute debris came sifting down, its presence in the atmosphere seeming little but time's flat taste and odour now. Haggard swore under his breath. He was shaken all right — why deny it to himself? — and beginning to feel sick at the stomach. To the devil with Black Jo and her robbers! And damn that boss of his, Judge Hubert Bracknell too! The judge had no moral right to keep on ranting that this case had gone on far too long. The man needed a bit more tolerance, and a few moments like these would give it to him. Yet, from the practical standpoint, Bracknell was right. He, Haggard, had spent too long getting nowhere on this case, and he was going to be much happier when Black Jo and her villains were behind bars. But there was many a slip between the cup and the lip and, even though he was pretty sure that the woman and her gang were holed up not many yards beyond where he stood now, any number of things could still go wrong and leave him dead and all his work in vain. The apparently collapsing roof not least among them!

Once more the ceiling was quiet. Haggard pressed on for a minute or so, still feeling his way with fingertips or the muzzle of his rifle, and he was soon aware of walking quite steeply uphill. Then the sound of distant voices came muttering into the chill of silence of the black tube that contained him. A sudden excitement bucked him up and took away his fear. He catfooted a few more paces, then was able to corner visibly to the left where the light renewed itself as a faint grey haze. Now he found himself looking towards a circle of silvery radiance — clearly a cavemouth — on the nearer side of which figures were sitting around the shadowy walls of a cave that had a small and almost smokeless juniper fire burning at the centre of its floor.

Haggard checked. He could smell

coffee and tobacco smoke, and somebody was playing a rather threadbare tune on what sounded like a homemade whistle. There was the cave he sought, and there were the Callard gangsters. He presumed the outlaws were all present, and knew that he would have to behave as if they were in any case. Though the possibility that somebody was missing — and might crop up as a threat to him at a later moment — was a risk that he would have to take. That particular hazard came the way of a lawman working alone all too often.

Gathering himself, Haggard prepared to dive straight in. Shock was the best weapon, and he reckoned that his gun-toting eruption into the cave would produce shock enough. Once he had disarmed the outlaws, he would be able to march them out of the cave, down the slope which he had earlier glimpsed beyond it, and round the nearby rockfaces to where he had left his horse and pack mule. The mule was carrying manacles among his gear, and it wouldn't take long to put the wrongdoers in chains. Nor would he have any gentlemanly scruples about it where Josephine Callard was concerned. She deserved to be locked into irons more than any member of her gang, and he intended to see that she got every scrap of what she deserved. Yes, he figured that he had it all clearly enough thought out and the need now was just to do it.

But then, paralysing in its force, a thunderous splitting noise issued from the rock-encased spaces to his rear, and air from the depths broke and rushed about him ominously. The roof had merely cracked and scattered a little debris before, but now it was obviously on the verge of breaking up and tumbling down in earnest. Slabs of stone began crashing to rest in his wake, and waves of detritus went rumbling and roaring down the darksome length of the tunnel floor up which he had so recently groped his uneasy way. He suspected that disaster had been impending along the roof of the passage for many a year, and he was instinctively certain that it had just now arrived. But what a moment to choose! The gods of ill-chance could not have picked a worse one! Here he was, poised before the biggest arrest of his career, and all at once the only certainty present was that he would die if he didn't get out of this collapsing passage at an even faster pace than he had planned. For the break-up had abruptly progressed to the roof directly above him, and lumps of stone more than big enough to brain him were already thudding down on either hand.

A rock brushed his left shoulder. That did it. He was dimly aware of a huge vitality exploding to life within him. One moment he stood yards back inside the crumbling passage, while the next found him almost literally flying through the air and entering the cave, where he dragged a booted foot through the fire and then collapsed upon his knees, conscious of dust swirling around him and the rifle still in his grasp going off with a roar. Blinking upwards, he saw male faces about him, jaws fallen and eyes bulging — the men perhaps suspecting that he was some form of supernatural visitor — and he sensed that they were badly startled and that all was far from lost despite his slightly premature arrival in the midst. Cocking his rifle anew, he mouthed a challenge — which struck him as rather inane in the circumstances — and was starting to rise again, when the muzzle of a revolver jarred against his left temple and a woman's voice, husky and superior, said: "Drop it — and get up slowly!"

Haggard let the Winchester clatter to the floor. Then he rose as the female commanded. Giving his left shoulder a push, she now ordered him to face her. This he did, conscious that further clouds of dust were roiling out of the tunnelmouth in the rear wall of the cave from which he had lately sprung.

The rumbling in the rock beyond also continued, but not for very long, and everything through there soon settled into quiet, though the odd thud or rattle told of loose stones that were still coming adrift and falling.

With the men previously seated around the walls now getting up and closing in upon her — and all more or less back to normal — the woman peered deep into Haggard's face and said: "Now let's see what we've got here!"

"Hot damn!" breathed a tall and exceptionally handsome man of thirty or so, who towered behind the female and gazed down on the prisoner with small eyes that were icy blue and wicked. "We've caught ourselves a lawman. And not just any old lawman either. Look at that badge, Jo! He's a deputy United States marshal."

"I'll tell you who he is," gravelled a short man standing on the captive's right, a blocky jaw thrusting and brows beetling towards the bridge of a pudgy nose. "I saw him a time or two when I was in San Angelo. That there's your very own Frank Haggard. He's Judge Bracknell's hangman. 'Twas him sent Billy Bonar through the trap last year!"

"Did you do that, Marshal?" the woman — undoubtedly Black Jo Callard herself — demanded.

"That was the sentence of the court," Haggard answered stonily. "I'm employed by the Judiciary, and paid to obey the orders of its officers. Yes, I put Billy Bonar to death. He was one of yours, I know. Be careful the rest of you don't end up sharing his fate!"

"Kill him," the tall man said. "He makes bad noises."

"We'll avenge Billy Bonar," Black Jo promised.

"Then do it," the tall man urged. "Or if you won't, leave it to me."

"What does he weigh?" the woman inquired.

"Eh?" The tall man frowned at her. "Hell, Jo, the questions you ask!

Around two hundred."

"Do you want to carry a body weighing two hundred pounds out to a grave on the prairie?" Black Jo asked. "I can't see it happening. You're a strong man, Chris Daggart, but not one who likes to exert himself more often than he's forced."

"She's got you pegged, Chris!" commented the stocky man who had just now identified the marshal, faintly jeering.

"Button your lip, Toms," Daggart ordered dangerously.

"Yes, be careful, Abel," the woman chided. "You know what Chris is like."

"Sure," Toms confided, not the least bit afraid, "he's a surly varmint. I don't know who'd win out if him and me pulled on each other."

"Don't talk it up, Abel!" the female gang-boss snapped. "You two are always bickering. We've got a job this afternoon, remember, and shall have to ride out shortly."

"How does that square with what

we've got on here, Jo?" asked another member of the woman's six-strong gang, a hulking, shaggy man, piggy-eyed and round-skulled. "It ought to be fixed before we leave. How if we plug the polecat and dump him in the corner for now? He ain't goin' to do more than bleed a little."

If only by association, Black Jo couldn't be too fussy about such matters, but she winced visibly nevertheless and a faintly disgusted expression touched her eyes, though this dissolved into a hard smile which also seemed to mask an underlying nature which, if carefully concealed, was of a much richer kind than her behaviour so far had suggested. But no alteration of expression could change the undeniable beauty of her face, with its classical nose and mouth, big violet eyes of an almond shape, and ivory forehead that was at once broad and tall. Her hair was the only spoiling feature in her good looks, for, jet black and shiny though it was, it had been tightly braided and pinned about her head in what Haggard saw as the banged fashion of the German housewife. If Black Josephine Callard had wished to be a more natural member of her sex — and seen looking beautiful as more important than anything else — there was little doubt that a better arrangement of her hair would have done much for her and perhaps changed her whole appearance almost out of recognition. Indeed, although he knew that he shouldn't acknowledge it — and was determined not to let his feelings influence his thinking in the slightest — Haggard was taken with her. As he looked down at her perfect shape and the manner in which her spun cotton trousers clung to her hips and thighs, he was conscious of a tightening in his solar plexus and a spasm of desire; and Black Jo, being all woman, whatever else she wasn't, picked up the impulse and shot him a quick and secret look, a faint catch audible in her breathing and touches of colour appearing in her cheeks. Then, as if in flat denial of all this subjectivity, she abruptly tilted her revolver upwards and pulled the trigger, nicking the lobe of the marshal's left ear ever so slightly, and she gazed at the piggy-eyed man with cold humour as the blood began to drip down from the wound and spatter the dust on the cave floor. "Bleed a little, Dan?" she inquired of the big man. "What kind of home did you have?"

"Aw, heck!" the large badman protested. "I know I'm kind of rough, Jo; but, like you always say, my heart's in the right place."

"Don't turn our stomachs, Ward!" Chris Daggart pleaded. "If you can't do better than that, don't talk at all." The tall man rubbed his jaw. "Tell you what, Jo."

"What?"

"Leave Dan Ward here to watch the lawman. We can hold up the Fort Stockton stage without his help."

Black Jo looked uncertain; then gave a quick nod and said: "Okay — why

16

not? The marshal will have to be tied up; but even so it would be wiser not to leave him here alone. We can do — what has to be done when we get back."

"Like making him dig his own grave?" Daggart suggested wolfishly.

"If you like," Black Jo said shortly. "So long as he's buried where his grave will never be found. When a Federal man gets murdered, the authorities take it hard."

"Is that meant to scare us?" Daggart wondered. "If this specimen is anything to go by, they're a mighty poor bunch."

"Well, Chris, he ain't goin' to get the chance," Toms reflected, "but I'd back his gun against yours any day."

The tall Daggart swung furiously on the much shorter Toms. "If I had the running of this gang, mister — "

"You don't, Chris," Black Jo reminded, her voice brittle. "You're man enough and to spare, but you're short on brains. You once had the running of this gang, but it was a very

17

poor job of it that you did."

"You can say that again, Jo!" declared a fourth member of the gang. This one hadn't spoken before. He was a young, curly-haired fellow, with small features and a sallow skin. One who looked a nice guy until the brutal twist of his mouth was seen along with the mean light in his eyes. "How many jobs did he find us? We rode broke from Shreveport to San Antone. It's not much fun foragin' for your grub. You surely brought money into our lives, Jo. Every job's been a good one, and Bonar was the only man we've lost. That was mostly his own fault too. I've got you down for a livin' wonder, Jo!"

"Thank you, Dilks," the woman said jauntily. "It's nice to be appreciated."

"Even if you do vanish away for weeks on end," a fifth man, big, dark and thoughtful, said dryly. "Real woman o' mystery, ain't you?"

"As I've told you before, Padman," Black Jo said smoothly, "the vanishing away, as you call it, is merely part of finding jobs for us to do. Don't start asking awkward questions again. You agreed to take my life and presence on trust. All suspicion was to be dropped."

"Quit it, Ike!" Daggart chuckled at Padman. "We're not to embarrass the lady. You know that. I dare swear our Jo has got a husband over Sheffield way. If I didn't see her — "

"You didn't!" Black Jo interrupted with a snap. "I think of you as my lieutenant, Chris. Who can I trust if I can't trust you?" She frowned at Daggart, her chin sinking into her red silk neckerchief.

"Leave it alone, Chris. Forget it! Don't be a trial. It doesn't follow that every woman who won't lie with you has a man stashed away in the next county. And leaving the gang for periods of time doesn't mean that she's up to anything mysterious or out of the ordinary."

"If you say so," Daggart said, just too submissively.

"Have I ever let any one of you boys

down in any way at all?" Black Jo asked hotly, her fine eyes challenging all present.

"In no way, Jo," the sixth and last member of her gang placated, deliberately drawing everybody's attention to his tallish, very thin figure, which gave the impression of being all weathered skin pulled tight over an extra large skeleton. "Like Dilks said: You're a livin' wonder, girl. I, for one, don't wanna know more than that." He scratched audibly at the seat of his canvas pants. "Reckon I'm lost to the rest of you right now. So help me, I do! What bothers me is how that lawman found out about us here, and what'd have happened if that tunnel hadn't damn nigh fallen in on him."

"They're very serious points you're making, Lance," the woman agreed, her voice pleasant enough again. "Not that the tunnel's falling in matters much. We've been expecting that to happen for a long time. But how this man Haggard learned about this hideout of ours does matter. We mustn't use it again after today. Though the fact he's here alone seems to suggest that he's the only one in the know."

"Marshal Haggard is known to be a lone wolf," Abel Toms said. "Some say he's not too trustin' of others. Others say he likes to keep the credit to himself. I've heard, too, he's just a hard-hearted bastard nobody can stomach. Maybe we should torture what we want to know out of the sidewinder. It'd be fittin'."

"He wouldn't talk," Daggart said dismissively.

"He would if I went to work on him," Toms promised brutally, his ugly face flushing with anger.

"Not again!" Black Jo protested. "You are a terrible pair! There will be no torture. Whatever Haggard knows will die with him. We shan't be using this place any more after today."

"Might be safer not to come back here at all," Daggart reflected. "We've got that old shack on the edge of the Edwards. I reckon that's as good a place as any to make our next home. It's a poky little hole, I know, but — "

"Suit yourself," Black Jo advised indifferently, when the tall man broke off, looking at her inquiringly. "We'll come back here, as already planned, and take care of Marshal Haggard. After that — I have other fish to fry."

"Does that mean you're having another spell away from us?" Daggart asked narrowly.

"Yes."

"I see."

"No, you don't, Chris," the woman said flatly. "You just think you do."

Daggart stirred angrily. "If you were a man, Jo — "

"You are a man," Black Josephine said with a chilling finality. "The world holds far too many of you. If I didn't have some regard for you, Chris — if only because of your usefulness to me — I'd have killed you long ago. I'm not boss here because I'm a woman. I'm boss here because I'm best with a gun. I'm capable of beating you to the draw, Chris, and of shooting straighter. Well you know it!"

"You're more than handy," Daggart admitted grudgingly. "I wouldn't want to put it to the test."

"Then just you remember that I'm always ready!" the woman snarled at him. "Chris, I've had enough of you, and this is your last warning. If you force me to shoot at you, I won't just crop your ear. It will be Dan Ward carrying you out to your grave. Understand?"

"What a storm in a teacup!" Daggart said disdainfully, but not too much so, for he obviously didn't want to nurse his pride into a new provocation. "Isn't it time we hossed up and got the hell out of here?"

"It is time," Black Jo agreed. "Let's go. All save you, Dan."

"Yeah," the large, piggy-eyed badman sniffed. "I'm to watch the lawman."

"The better part of it, I'd say," Black Jo observed.

"You may say," Dan Ward grumbled. "Do I have to, Jo? You don't get proper protected if I ain't around."

"You have to, Dan," the woman said firmly. "I can see I'm going to have to make you men mind. You're beginning to take advantage."

"Not me, gal!" Ward protested. "Not me!"

"Then do as you're told."

"Yes'm," the big man said obediently, drawing his revolver and thrusting the weapon's muzzle into Haggard's face. "I got the weight."

Black Jo gave a curt little nod. Then she spun her own pistol back into its holster. After that, beckoning, she walked out of the cave's front entrance, and Chris Daggart and the rest of the villains followed on.

Dan Ward let his colleagues get out of earshot. Then, glaring at Haggard, he uttered a low cry and otherwise gave vent to his feelings, swinging over a left hook that caught the marshal on the side of the jaw with force enough to have staggered an ox.

Unfortunately, Haggard was no ox. He fell through a scarlet flash into the black pit at the bottom of the world.

2

IT must have been several minutes later when Haggard regained consciousness. He came to himself muttering and shaking his head. The second was a painful process which he soon stopped. Then, looking down, he saw that his hands had been bound at the wrists in front of him, and realized that he had been propped in a sitting position against the wall of the cave on the right of the entrance. Dan Ward was standing over him, chin in hand and expression thoughtful. "Had to hit you," he said.

"I don't see why," Haggard rubbered out dazedly, believing for a moment that his jaw was broken, but soon discovering that its joints had been no more than wrenched.

"Had to tie your hands together," Ward explained. "I didn't have you pegged for the kind of guy who'd just stand there and let me do it."

Haggard gave a twisted smile. "And there was me thinking it was all for love of the girl."

"W — what?" the big man spluttered. "She's young."

"You're old?"

"I'm thirty-eight."

He looked older than that, by a year or two at least, but Haggard had sense enough not to tell him so, for he had already made up his mind to work on what he judged to be the ugly villain's weakness — love for a much younger and far superior woman — since even a man with his hands bound could sometimes manage a trick or two when a captor such as his was off guard. "Thirty-eight, eh? Well, that's just nice in my opinion. A girl often stands a better chance of happiness with an older man. Push your suit, Dan. Where's the harm?"

"Aw, I'm nothin' much," Ward said

with surprising humility. "Jo Callard is a lady."

"Jo Callard is an outlaw, my friend."

"I'm not your friend," the large villain gritted, "and you're not mine! Don't you bad mouth her, lawman. 'Cos if you do, I'll kick you apart right now!"

"Simmer down!" Haggard urged. "I was just stating the fact. You're an outlaw, mister, and so is she. That makes you equals. Neither one of you is better than the other."

"Stuff!" Ward retorted. "Have you seen the books she reads?"

"How could I have done that?" Haggard wondered. "I never set eyes on the woman before today." He fixed the big man's gaze with his own. "I'm surprised Black Jo reads when she's around you guys."

"She don't," Ward clarified. "Not more than the local newspapers, like the rest of us. It was what I saw when she once let her gunny sack fall. I helped her pick up what dropped out. I saw books with leather covers, jewellery, foreign cigarettes, and a lace handkerchief. The kind of things a real lady likes to keep about her." He turned his head and spat into the still flickering remains of the ploughed up fire, his spittle hissing briefly on its arrival among the embers. "Just look at her, man! Was she a pup off that old black bitch? You know better than that! She's a well-born girl, educated and such, meant for a good life. Tell me I'm wrong!"

"I won't tell you that," Haggard said, recognising that layers of personal interest, concerning Black Jo Callard — and additional to those which he had originally seen in this rather unique case — were being added to the mystery of the woman all the time; for he was no longer thinking of her purely as a female crook but as an extraordinary person who had flouted the law for reasons that he could not as yet even start to guess at. "You certainly speak well for the lady, Dan. You're mighty fond of her, aren't you?"

"In a fatherly sort of way I guess."

"You burn for her."

"That ain't nice."

"It's natural enough, Dan," Haggard commented gravely. "We all fall in love at least once. It's hard when you've seen a woman, know she's the one you must have, but know, too, that you can never have her. That's a pain to end all pains, Dan. You mustn't suffer it. Go after the girl!"

"You keep callin' me Dan!" Ward complained, suddenly angry again. "Told you, lawman. I ain't no friend of yours. No, by cracky! You want some more proof? Hell, boy!" He reached down, both hands slapping back and forth, and his leathery palms made contact with the prisoner's cheeks about a dozen times before he stepped back, breathing a little hard and with teeth bared and eyes blazing. "Do you believe me now, skunk? No? How about this then?" And he lashed out with his right foot, the toe of his boot burying itself under Haggard's ribs and finding his spleen, the pain of it tipping him on to his left side, an inert, semi-conscious figure with bile dribbling from the corners of his mouth. "Have you got it now? I ain't your friend, blast your eyes! You keep your mouth off Josephine!"

Just able to hear Dan Ward, though the man's words registered only at the boundary of his understanding, the marshal went on lying motionless — indeed he couldn't have managed much more than that had he tried — and he was aware that the big man went on looking down at him in continued resentment. But Ward, with all his emotion and viciousness, was no mental giant, and his concentration span was limited. Muttering curses to himself, he finally turned away from the doubled body of his victim and went clumping towards the way out of the cave. "You must get over it as best as you can," he mumbled across his shoulder. "You ain't so tough, hombre!" After that he stepped outside and went shuffling down the incline beyond.

The now slowly recovering Haggard listened intently as the sounds of the big villain's descent receded. He was amazed at the other's folly in leaving him totally unguarded, though he had realized that Dan Ward was emotionally sick and not altogether responsible just now. But that was what love did to a man, and what the marshal had set out to exploit — with this far better than expected result. He had been granted his chance, and must now make the most of it.

Haggard dredged up all his willpower. Then he rolled onto his face. Now he began squirming towards the almost burned out remnants of the fire. Renewed spasms of pain brought him up short, but he assimilated these and refused to register any more. There was iron in him — because there had to be. He had ridden out to do a job, and he would do it to the limit. Not because Judge Bracknell demanded it, or because the Office of the United States Marshal for the Southwest expected it, but because he had a true professional man's pride in his work and record. Not to mention that other little matter known as staying alive. For he had always held that a fellow was a long time dead, and the grave best left to the worms.

He got himself moving again. Seconds later he reached what was left of the fire. Soot and half burned sticks lay scattered, and he looked for flame with a squinting eye, but saw none. He felt a wave of disappointment, and his resolve weakened for all the power of his good intentions. It would have been easy to give up in that moment — in the plausible belief that what he had set himself to do had been rendered impossible by circumstance, since the fire seemed dead in all that mattered. But, disregarding what appeared to be the fact of it, he raised his head and began blowing gently on a juniper twig from which grey smoke curled thinly. A last spark flickered, and heat manifested as an orange glow that gradually deepened until a tiny flame burst from the wood and spread into other fragments of combustible material about it.

Heartened by this small success, Haggard forced out his hands beyond the bonds that held his wrists and drew in more of the partially burned twigs to feed his central fire. He kept puffing through his lips at the flames until he had built the minor blaze that he sought; then, once sure that his little fire would burn long and hotly enough to fulfil his purpose, he forced his wrists apart as far as they would go — which wasn't all that far — and pushed his bonds into the flames. The heat seared his wrists, and a new and different sort of agony filled him. He watched the hairs frizzle up on his pores, and the skin itself soon turned an ugly red and began to flake and peel. But, skinned and blistered though he quickly found a part of his hands and the lower joints of his arms to be, he persisted in what he was doing and saw the cord that held his wrists together start to scorch and burn. Even so, it took more than a minute for the flames to achieve any real amount of dissolution and he was only just hanging on to his resolve when he perceived that the fire had eaten deep enough into the weave for muscle power to do the rest. Thus, shutting his eyes, he lifted his arms and jerked his hands apart, the cord about his wrists breaking instantly and his upper limbs falling weakly to the floor. Then he knelt there, briefly paralysed, and the sweat trickled down his face.

Presently Haggard climbed to his feet. Gritting his teeth against the pain which emanated from his burned flesh, he turned an ear in the direction of the cavemouth, seeking even the faintest sound which might indicate Dan Ward's return or near presence. But there was nothing; just the same old silence that had marked the man's absence for several minutes now. So, desiring to arm himself if he could, Haggard took further advantage of the badman's tardiness to move around the cave and ferret into the warbags and blanket-rolls which Black Jo and her outlaws had left lying in the place; but he found little of interest — and certainly no firearm — and was forced to the conclusion that the gangsters had more sense than to leave anything that mattered behind them. They had even taken his own rifle with them and, while he had a gunbelt stowed away on his horse, he saw no hope of being able to challenge Dan Ward with a shooting-iron in the near future. This also meant, of course, that he must try to avoid giving Ward the opportunity to fire at him, since an unarmed man almost always came off second best against a fellow with a Colt to hand. It was discouraging, yes — but the initiative nevertheless remained with him for now.

It occurred to the marshal that he

could be worrying too much over details that might not prove relevant to what was actually happening. He had kept his ears lifting all the time that he had been in full possession of himself, but he still had no idea of where Ward had gone or what the man was doing. He must attempt to remedy that before anything else; so he stepped up to the threshold of the cave and peered out — and then down — for a considerable scree-slope fell below the entrance to the hideout and he had a wide view of it and the country beyond; but of Dan Ward there was no immediate sign, and he was soon more than half convinced that the big outlaw had simply gone off and left him.

Then a small movement about half way down the dun coloured acclivity tugged at his eye, and he made out Ward's big shape seated on a boulder. The man had his back to the cave and was engaged in the rather futile but rhythmic exercise of picking up stones with one hand and casting them away from him again with the other. He appeared to be trying to land his missiles in the strip of aspens and denser greenery that ran across the base of the slope, first enclosing a pond, and then seeming to provide a perspective for the brown-green miles of the prairie beyond. Every so often, he would raise his eyes and try to throw further, as if to send some part of himself into the hazy escarpments of the far distance, where striated skies of buttermilk and brighter blue hovered above the confluence of the Pecos river and the Rio Grande itself. The loneliness of it all was like an aching presence, and it seemed to match Dan Ward's mood exactly. There could be little doubt that the villain had forgotten both where he was and the responsibility with which he had been charged. It ought not to be difficult to by-pass him. Haggard certainly wasn't looking for a fight in his present condition. But then he realized that Ward knew where the back exit to the cave came out — and therefore the spot from which the marshal had commenced creeping up on Black Jo and her gang — so, when he did discover, as sooner or later he must, that his prisoner had escaped, he would know within a little where Haggard had left his horse and pursue accordingly. There was, regretfully, no choice for it. One way or another, Dan Ward would have to be removed from the picture before the marshal could give further attention to striking off the bigger names on his list.

Haggard left the cave and set off down the slope. He was aware that his movement was precipitate to say the least of it. For he had no clear plan in mind as to how the big villain was to be eliminated. The only sure factor was that whatever kind of attack he made would have to be closely physical. If he could crack Ward on the head with a stone, all to the good, and even if he could only manage to knock the man unconscious with a lump of thrown rock, it would do equally well. But he hoped to goodness that he didn't get forced into a fistfight with Ward. Normally, he would have been confident of easily overcoming the big guy, but with hands as badly burned as his were now, he reckoned landing a blow with full force on a chin like the rogue's would probably hurt him as much as it did his foe. Thus, if at all possible, he must avoid fisticuffs. But he had an uneasy feeling that it could not be done; so he began steeling himself for the worst.

His steps getting progressively slower as he neared Dan Ward, the marshal also set his feet down with an increasing care; but, no matter what the lightness with which he put his soles down, the loose material underfoot gave out its same old metallic rattling as bits and pieces of it slid this way and that. The noise seemed loud and disturbing to Haggard, and he was amazed that it didn't impinge upon the ears of the despondent badman, but Ward went on looking to his front and gave no sign of having heard anything at all beyond the small noises made by his own doings.

Doubling low, in fear that the villain must hear something amiss and peer round as the man creeping up got even closer, Haggard altered course into a zig zag approach to gain cover from some of the larger rocks in the vicinity, and it was now — with the intensification of the marshal's mental effort more than anything else — that the outlaw showed his first signs of emerging from his dismal reverie and becoming conscious again of the ground about him. Yet, for all that, Haggard had got to within six yards of the man before Ward's pudding of a head drew to full alert on his short neck and he turned his chin abruptly over his right shoulder.

The badman's stare just about missed the marshal, who had contrived to duck with the greatest haste. Keeping his breathing checked and jaw tilted, Haggard heard Dan Ward mutter questioningly. Then came sounds which told him that the big man had stood up and was facing round. After that slow, crunching footfalls warned that the outlaw had begun climbing back up the slope in the most watchful of fashions. Now, somewhat daring, Haggard glanced round the top of the boulder which concealed him and saw Ward looming on his left. The man was ascending with pistol drawn and, from peering over to his right, he suddenly swept his eyes back in the opposite direction at a pace for which the marshal had made no prior allowance, and Haggard realized, as he settled into hiding again, that he had been at least glimpsed on this occasion.

There was a long, listening pause, which again emphasized the total silence normal to this spot.

"Who is that?" the big villain asked all at once, his tones tentative.

Haggard remained completely still and hushed.

"Know you're there."

The marshal slowly released his pent up breath; for, with all its attempted certainty, the outlaw's voice had still held a hint of doubt about the matter.

"That you, Marshal?" the crook demanded, his tones thickened by an abrupt suspicion. "How the unholy hollerin' hell did you manage to — ?"

Haggard grew taut. The outlaw was climbing fast now and must spot the marshal's crouched figure at any moment.

It was necessary to think at lightning speed. Haggard realized that he must divert the big man's attention for long enough to rise up and jump on him; so the marshal grabbed a lump of scree and sent it flying sideways, and it landed with a small crash about twenty yards beyond him and created a brief slide amidst the layers of debris where it had come down. Popping his head up as this disturbance began, Haggard saw that Ward's face had already turned towards the fairly distant noise and that the outlaw's gaze was missing him entirely.

The body had to react as swiftly as the mind at this juncture and, in what amounted to a single clean movement, Haggard jacked himself erect and bounded on top of the rock before him. Then he launched out at the big guy, who was poised for trouble not more than three yards away, and he hit the villain in the middle of the chest with raised forearms and sent him staggering backwards.

Floundering, Ward fought to recover himself, bringing his revolver up in the process and pulling the trigger; but he had been too surprised to take any real aim and his bullet flew past the marshal's left cheek and went on to slap audibly against the tall rockface in which Black Jo's hideout was situated.

Haggard went for his man again. Regardless of the pain it caused him, he let fly with his fists, battering Ward about the jaw and temples, and the outlaw went reeling to his rear a second time, his pistol banging skywards now as he flung up his arms in an effort to retain his balance against the tripping presence of a reef of stone at his heels.

Once more the marshal dived in, his forearms pounding, and Ward staggered and gyrated past the boulder on which he had originally been seated and into a settling area of the slope beyond. The big man had lost all control of his heavy frame by now and, when he arrived on a jagged brink over a deep gash in the acclivity which had not been visible to Haggard from his earlier position above and behind the outlaw, he could do nothing to prevent himself from falling. Down he went, uttering a terrified cry, and his disappearance from the marshal's sight was closely followed by a crash that spoke of his heavy landing amidst more stone below.

Haggard dragged to a halt, his lungs pumped hard, and he had to allow a moment to recover his breath before going up to the brink of the drop and looking over. Ward was lying on his back amidst scree and sharp rocks about thirty feet below. The man's eyes were shut, but his jaw had sagged and a pool of blood was forming around the back of his head. From this distance above, he appeared dead, and Haggard would have put money on this being so, for the drop was a considerable one and the big man had fallen anyhow at all. Well, whatever the exact truth of Ward's physical state — and Haggard had no intention of trying to climb down into the gulch to ascertain it — the outlaw was certainly out of the reckoning for now and could be left lying against whatever ministrations his gangster colleagues should see as necessary when they eventually found him. The marshal's remaining responsibility here — as he saw it — was to get clear for the moment and return to his horse and mule, where he would be able to rearm himself and then work out a new plan to capture the outlaw gang, which was now all too fully alerted to his presence in the field against them and would be on guard as never before. To hang around here, whatever his motives or other concerns, could only bring him more trouble. And he had had enough of that for the present, thank you.

3

HAGGARD'S walk around the rockface, back to the place where he had left his horse and pack mule, was a much longer one than he had anticipated on his earlier experience of the neighbourhood, and he was not helped by the pains that kept cramping into his body from the spot where Dan Ward had kicked him under the ribs. His burned wrists and hands also played him up. These injuries had no effect on his leg movements, of course, but the pain from them was so great that it lowered his vitality to the extent that he felt almost completely worn out by the time he rejoined the animals on the greensward where he had left them tied into a clump of box elder not far from the main stream of the Pecos.

Freeing the animals, Haggard made

to mount up, intending to leave the area down the western bank of the river; but he had no sooner got astride his horse and turned to gather the mule's lead rein than he fell out of his saddle and landed on his hands and knees beside the old black stud. The impact made him sick, and he saw blood in the vomit. Fearing that he might have a serious internal injury, he crept over to the river and thrust his face into the river's cool flow, knowing that he could die out here if anything was badly amiss inside him — for expert medical help was miles away and beyond any power of his to summon — but, after he had drunk a pint or two of water and kept his hands and wrists immersed in the Pecos for an hour or so, he began to feel a lot better and was able to withdraw from the water's-edge and return to his animals.

Still unsure of himself, Haggard stepped up for the second time and managed to hold his seat without difficulty. His bend towards his mule also caused him no problem and, feeling no worse than a mite light-headed, he gigged up and began following the riverbank southwards as bereft of any real plan as at any time that day. In fact he realized that his only intention now was to get as far away from Black Jo Callard's hideout as he could before nightfall, then find some sheltered corner and lie up in his blankets until he either died or his strength came back. At the minute he was too weak to even think, and there was no more fight in him. He had done pretty well, and would have heartily congratulated another man on what he had himself achieved earlier in the day, but he guessed it was all part of the job and that only he would ever know what it had cost him. That's what you got for being a riding marshal. Small pay and less appreciation. Oh, to hell with it! In his experience, every man believed he had lived the hardest life that ever was. Only God could judge — if He did exist!

Jogging along at little better than a walking pace, Haggard went on following the waters of the river for the next quarter of an hour. Then, glancing to his right, he saw the rockface which contained Black Jo's cave and the upper part of the slope beneath it. He wondered indifferently whether the apparently dead Dan Ward had perhaps recovered in the past hour or two or if the ugly badman were still lying with his head in that pool of blood, stiffening as the day aged and blown by the horseflies that flew in off the plains.

It was as if the thought itself produced a violent reaction from the land to the west. For a line of rifles suddenly started to flash and bang from a line of rocks that stood about half way between the familiar slope facing the prairie and the river itself. Haggard could hardly grasp that he was the object of the shooting, but he woke up to the fact sharply enough as a bullet thudded into his cantle and others hissed and spat around him. Jarred out of his lassitude, he let go of his mule's lead rein and kicked high, striking hard with his spurs. His horse surged into a gallop, and the marshal lowered his face towards the brute's mane and simply let it go. They moved along at a splendid pace for around half a minute — the rifles banging more and more raggedly in their wake — and Haggard was pretty sure that he had almost outrun the attempt to gun him down, when his horse broke stride momentarily and gave an agonised little squeal which echoed strangely.

Haggard's heart sank. That sound had been a cry from the spirit. His horse had just received a mortal wound. He could already feel the animal's strength ebbing. It would go on literally until it dropped — of that he was certain — but, for all its natural bravery, it could not live much longer and would probably set him afoot within the easy compass of his enemies.

For the people shooting at him from

back there had to be Black Jo and her men, no doubt recently returned from their hold-up. Nor was it unlikely, in view of this interception, that they were being to some extent guided and inspired by Dan Ward, who could well be still alive and taking an active part in the lawman's latest discomfiture. If that were the right word to use. Since the marshal looked like dying here after all, and death was rather more than an embarrassment.

Increasingly desperate, Haggard continued raking at his mount's flanks and knew that he was at least nearing the limit of rifle shot, when his horse was hit for the second time. He heard the slug pass over his own right shoulder and saw it punch a black hole behind the brute's right ear. Mercifully brained, the old stallion dropped in its stride, spinning to the left on the ground and carrying its rider with it in the impetus of the same whirling motion towards the edge of the Pecos, which was only a few yards away. The dead horse splashed into the river, and the marshal plunged in behind it. Both sank to the bottom of the water, but only Haggard started to rise again.

Breaking surface, the marshal gulped air. Then, treading water, he gazed around him. Instinctively he struck out for the shore — which was only a few feet away — but had yet to put his hands upon the brink, when he saw figures running in his direction from the rocks that had concealed the riflemen. He realized that his hunters would have him in full view the moment he pulled himself on to dry land, and shooting at him then would be a much easier business than it had been when he was on horseback. Indeed, he felt sure that the badmen would put paid to him with their first volley.

No, he would be a wiser man if he stayed in the water. While his enemies would be able to see him plainly enough in the river — and could fire on him as readily as a swimmer as they could ashore — he at least had the presence of a fast current to help him downstream and could always duck under the surface if the bullets became too plentiful or too accurate. True, runners ashore could easily keep up with his waterborne progress southwards — and he did not perceive how his swim was to end well — but he could think of nothing else to do right now and staying in the river might at least keep him alive a bit longer.

Swimming strongly away from the bank, Haggard headed out into the really deep and fast water of the middle flow. This put more than forty yards between him and the people who soon appeared on the western shore opposite. He made out Black Jo's slighter figure among the men, and saw her gesticulating and heard her shouting. Then the rifles began to bang at him again, and slugs plopped into the water all around his head; but, between the swirling forces of the current and his own efforts, Haggard was not a sitting duck and came to no harm.

The bullets went on coming — for Black Jo and company were nothing if not persistent — and the marshal did take shelter under the surface from time to time; but these dives were not particularly necessary to his safety and he soon began to feel quite confident where he had been despairing before. He hoped that the gangsters would soon accept that his escape was now more than possible and give up their pursuit along the riverbank, yet they continued to stay with him and their presence — no more than a mild irritation to start with — ended up as downright annoyance. But their determination only whetted his own, and he steeled himself to survive in the river until after darkness fell — when his ultimate escape ought to become a certainty.

Possessed of a real respect for Black Jo's intelligence, Haggard found it difficult to understand why the woman and her followers could not see the obvious, but they went plodding on along the shore with the same tenacity as the minutes passed by and he began to regard them as fools. Yet it wasn't so very long before he learned that the only foolishness present was his own, for the flow of the Pecos started to lose its force and began to spread into lagoons and narrow waterways between the muddy, reed-tufted islands of what was soon visible as an extensive marsh. Here the advantage was at once restored to the hunters, and it occurred to the marshal that the persistence of the gangsters, short of blind doggedness, had been based on knowledge that he didn't have. Now they could enter this swampy place and either knock him on the head and fish him out or shoot him from close range — with the accent on the latter course, he suspected. It just went to prove how careful a man always had to be when he started feeling sure of himself.

Haggard kept to the middle of the water as a matter of policy. The rifles had ceased shooting at him with any regularity long ago — though this was probably more due to shortage of ammunition than despair of skills — and he took advantage of the dearth of gunshots to raise himself up in the river and attempt to assess the scene ahead for any possibility of continued flight that the marsh might have to offer him after all. So far as he could be certain of it, there was a deep water channel flowing a little left of centre through the boggy jungle of brown reed and mudbanks which formed the perhaps unapproachable heart of the marsh and, if he could stay in that, he might be able to swim clear through this obstruction in the river's course and come out at the other side on another open stretch of the Pecos.

It was a chance all right, and worthy of his renewed efforts. Haggard steered himself towards the sluggish waterway that he wished to follow, but the liquids that supported him at this point suddenly ran fleet and forced him to scramble out of the river and up the face of a low sandbank. The channel for which he had been aiming was on the other side of this and just in sight through a screen of green reeds and fat brown bulrushes, so it appeared that a very short journey over land must now be made.

The sandbank was dry and solid enough, and it gave Haggard no trouble to claw his way to the top of it. Checking on the flat, he glanced back and round, praying that he was no longer visible to his hunters; but he saw at once that the opposite was true and, noting that guns were already levelled at him again, propelled himself back into motion at an explosive rate.

The rifles puffed and slugs laced an angry pattern about Haggard. Sand kicked up around his racing feet, and his wet garments were whipped more than once by lead. He plunged into the reeds, trampling stalks, and stems of a more mushy kind split as bullets ripped them and sent pith splashing.

Then he was conscious of flights of frightened marsh birds, duck, geese, teal and the like, blasting upwards out of the marsh and darkening the red light of the westering sun with the fitful movements of their soaring and banking shapes. Still the hissing lead sought him but, holding on to his nerve, Haggard cleared the tallest of the reeds and reached the water again. Diving through the dully glistening surface of the channel and arrowing deep into the muddy layer of liquid at the bottom of the waterway, he found himself half drowned by the lung-emptying effects of his haste, and he kicked over and came up again as swiftly as he could, wallowing on his back as he once more broke through into the air and gulping at the sky. His eyes dimmed, and he was filled with weakness. This was getting too much; he'd taken just all he could stand. Surely to goodness he was now lost behind marsh growth and no longer under the barrels of those guns. There had to be a respite!

He started swimming again, using the breaststroke, and only the top of his head from the nostrils upwards was above the surface. He seemed to be safe for the moment, since the shape of the marsh had carried his hunters on the solid ground to the west of him at least eighty yards from this channel. Slowing, he let his natural buoyancy raise his head and shoulders above the surface, and was allowing the current there to bear him forward, when fear chilled through him again; for, against all expectation, a rifle went off at a still short distance to his rear and water fountained beside his left shoulder. No, he could not believe it! Yet the even closer arrival of a second bullet compelled him so to do, and he tipped over and plunged, swimming under the surface after that towards the tall reeds of the shoreline on his right.

Coming to the top once more, he sent his gaze searching back — through a gap in the growth behind him — towards the last of the bank which followed the river's straighter course. Where could the rifleman be? The make up of the swampy area around here should now be protecting the swimmer entirely. But then he saw branches shake at the top of a cottonwood tree, on the outward turn of the western bank, and he realized that one of Black Jo's villains had climbed the tree and thus obtained an elevated firing position from which he should be able to cover the greater part of the present waterway for a fair distance ahead.

Yet, as his own view of the cottonwood was cut off by the apparently converging reed clumps on the shoreline behind him, Haggard was reasonably sure that, so long as he kept as near as possible to the reeds adjacent, he was invisible to the marksman and could progress safely for the moment. After that, reverting to the less tiring overarm stroke, he swam steadily forward with the current and the slow twist and turn of the marshland waterway gradually bore him through the swamp and down towards the expected egress at its southern end.

The marshal saw high banks and a hardening of the view before him. He felt the waters deepen and gather force as they funnelled in towards the main channel of the Pecos again, and the familiar tensions of the day — reduced for a good part of an hour now — tightened again inside his chilled frame and he started to wonder where and when his new reception by Black Jo and her gang would commence. Far beyond the normal limit of his strength — since his energies had time after time been sucked almost dry by events — he was light-headed again and responding to patterns of bodily motion which he had earlier impressed upon his mind. To his imagination, death was becoming rather desirable, for he felt that he needed rest more than any other man in the entire history of the world, and death was rest at its most profound; but he was still no jibber and forced himself to think of only the correct things to do, since the evening was here and sunset far advanced. As he had told himself before, if he could stay alive until darkness had fallen, he should be able to dodge the gang in the thickest of the night and ultimately get away. It remained a matter of enduring to the absolute limit. He could — and would — do it.

Yet, for all his toughness of mind, he seemed to be drifting — just drifting. Then a gun spoke, the explosion whacking out in the smoky hush of the hour, and Haggard felt speeding metal lance at the base of his throat, where the flesh protecting his carotid artery joined the big muscle which lay across the top of his left shoulder, and he realized, as his body heaved up waist-high out of the water in shock, that he had been more badly hurt than at any time previously, though the passing slug had done no worse than cut deeply enough to bleed him quite a lot. He was aware then of sliding back and down into the river, generally numbed and enveloped by the spreading stain of his own blood.

He touched the bottom erect, and slowly spun and wobbled there, and the undertow claimed him and carried him aside. As he started to rise — at a pace critical to his breathing — his crown made contact with loose dirt and roots and he knew that he had surfaced in the growth along the water's-edge. He hung there, gasping harshly to stay alive — but also convinced that he could not be seen now by the person who had shot at him — and, with his head surrounded by reeds, picked up more of the excited shouting that he had earlier heard after he and his dead horse had tumbled into the river.

"You got him that time, Daggart!" a male voice rasped triumphantly through the increasing gloom of this sunken place. "He went down like a stone!"

"He sure seemed to get it fair and

square, Padman," Daggart's brighter tones agreed, though a trifle uncertainly. "Can't be sure of anything. That marshal's got more tricks to him than a waggonload of monkeys!"

"You hit him all right, Chris," Black Jo Callard's voice observed, "but I don't think you killed him."

"I hope not!" seethed the voice of Dan Ward, offering conclusive proof that he was still alive and active. "That long bastard is my meat!"

"I can't see a trace of him, Jo," another speaker said. "Look at all that blood driftin' downstream too. If you ask me, he went down dead-as-a-doornail, and he ain't going to come up again before he bloats out."

"Maybe, Dilks," the woman said.

Her voice was much nearer to the listener now, and it wasn't long before Haggard heard footfalls approaching the spot where the river had delivered him into hiding. Weak and shocked to the core, he groped mentally for what to do about it. The light was still adequate to see by, and he was far from perfectly hidden. He reckoned that his head could easily be spotted by anybody standing opposite him on the bank just beyond this fringe of reeds, and he was convinced that he would shortly be discovered if he didn't take some further kind of action to put himself out of sight.

The marshal threw the whole of his imagination into it, but no inspiration came. The only idea that entered his mind was the oldest one of all for a man cornered in his present situation. Carefully lifting his right arm out of the water, he snapped off a dead reed; then, putting the broken end in his mouth, he nipped off the remains of the flower that had once decorated the growth and began settling lower and lower into the water, finally submerging his upturned face to a depth of about two feet and leaving the opened tip of his stalk in the air. Breathing in this fashion, for all the things said in its favour, was difficult in the extreme; but it could be managed; and he crouched there close to the bank, eyes popping and vital organs seriously starved of oxygen as he sucked thinly at the atmosphere above. He was often on the verge of panic, but necessity knew no choice, and he employed all his self-discipline to hold him motionless on the floor of the reedbed, while the minutes of his torture dragged by, each like a separate eternity.

Finally Haggard could see no point to suffering like this any longer. Deaf and blind to what was happening in the world outside the river, it was imperative that he find out what was going on, and he could do that only by lifting his head above water again. There was risk involved in that, and could be no moment that was surely safe. It was necessary to just take his chance and do it. So, very carefully still, he eased his torso upwards again until his head broke surface, then crouched there for a long moment while his ears drained and his senses adjusted to their normal functions.

He listened intently now and peered deeply into the enclosing gloom. Nothing. Just the sound of the river and other noises natural to the marsh.

Shivering in every fibre, he stayed there and stayed there, fearing a trap, but everything remained as quiet and still as before, and at last, throwing his redundant caution to the wind, he stood up on the bed of the river, turned, and waded to the bank. Throwing himself upon the brink, he scrambled his way stiffly ashore and lay gasping for a while in the waterside grass. He was still bleeding from the injury to the base of his neck, and he went on hurting internally too, while his nicked ear and the burns to his hands and wrists also stung and added to his suffering. It had all been one hell of an experience, but it seemed to be over for now, and he was safe. It was amazing how the most dire and terrifying situations could often resolve themselves in the simplest and quietest of fashions. Short of falling to a bullet, he was more likely now to die of pneumonia. This end to the day's almost incessant violence he had never foreseen.

Just then, he could not explain how, he was conscious of being watched. Turning his head across his shoulder, he peered into the dusk which cloaked a stand of timber about fifty yards back from the water's-edge. He could see nothing, but there was somebody there all right. He knew that he ought to be afraid, yet wasn't in the least. The watcher meant him no harm; quite the reverse indeed; for he sensed a wondering fondness in the stare, and got the further impression that the spirit behind it was female.

Haggard's brow knitted. This made no sense. Nor could he explain the sudden warmth in his heart. "Jo!" he called softly.

There was no response; but then he hadn't expected one.

He rose, still looking towards the trees, but hadn't the strength to do more. "Jo!" he repeated.

A dead branch cracked in the darkness of the trees. Perhaps a foot had pressed upon it. Haggard couldn't tell.

4

IT was at about that time that the most uncomfortable night of Frank Haggard's life began. His two or three hours of constant soaking in the river had softened his body and taken all the warmth out of it, and his sodden clothing permitted no chafing on the surface to bring back a healthy tingling to his oil-drained skin. Had the atmosphere been in any sense a cold one, he could not have stayed active for long once out of the river; but, luckily, the nights this far south — and coming into the late spring — were not particularly cold, though the vapour-hung airs close to the marsh and this deep into the valley of the Pecos were cool enough to bring constant chatter to the teeth of a wet man.

To further compound matters, near

exhaustion as he was, Haggard realized from the start that he would not be able to walk far, which was a terrible drawback — since he needed above all to return to the country where he had let go of his pack mule and attempt to find the animal again, for he required the dry clothing and such that it was carrying as part of his gear — and thus, as he was so restricted, he was forced to search around in the area where he had emerged from the river for a sheltered spot to curl up and try to generate enough body warmth to get him through the night. But hard as he sought, in the daze of fatigue that afflicted him, he shambled slowly northwards around the shores of the marsh without finding any place to put his head down and cover himself with grass or foliage. If he could have found a cave it would have been a real help, and a deep, mossy hollow might also have served, but there was nothing; and he was in the ultimate stages of exhaustion and despondency — and ready to lie as he fell, whatever the outcome of that — when he had one of those pieces of saving luck that occasionally come to the deserving. For he stumbled on a place where a reedcutter had been at work and discovered a stack of dry stems that seemed to him just then as good a potential covering for his icy flesh as any on the face of the earth.

Attacking the reed stack feet-first and a little above ground level, Haggard worked his way into the thatching material, ignoring the weight of the stalks above him — and the risk that he might get smothered if the whole lot slipped sideways across his face — and his body temperature at once began to rise, responding no doubt to the force of the burrowing exercise which he had imposed upon his legs, and presently he fell into a slightly delirious sleep that was filled with vividly coloured dreams and the hours of darkness passed for him in a kind of nightmare from which he emerged into the dawnlight.

He lay there feeling less than human. He was stiff as never before, and ached the same, while his various hurts felt little better than they had last evening, but his garments had all but dried on him and his instinct told him that he would be able to move with some purpose once more. He had survived the night, and could look forward to the warmth of the day. If grossly uncomfortable at the moment, he wasn't actually ill, and he should be able to help himself considerably — whatever circumstances he had to meet — before the darkness came again. Just so long as he didn't cross paths with Black Jo's gangsters any more, and could put some food into his belly. It was all a matter of finding that mule of his; for there was bread and jerky in a saddlebag, coffee too, not to mention lucifers and ammunition that he could break open to start a quick fire. Oh, the thought of warmth — real warmth — and a lining on his belly! When last came to last, the necessities were all that mattered.

The marshal began to ease himself out of the stacked rushes. He kicked gently with his feet and crept slowly backwards on his elbows. Aside from considering his own immediate safety, Haggard didn't wish to leave too many signs of his presence around, and he eventually pulled clear of the reedcutter's pile without leaving any real trace of the use he had made of it. Then, brushing himself down, he lurched away from the reed pile and soon injected a little determination into his steps as he resumed his path northwards, the morning grey and misty about him, waterfowl honking at him overhead, and the muddy smell of the swampy ground adjacent thick in his nostrils.

Rounding the remainder of the marsh took less time than Haggard expected; but, once he had started up country from the cottonwood out of whose top branches the rifleman had tried to nail him while he was swimming southwards yonder, he was amazed at how far down the river he had come from the spot where he had first entered the water yesterday. It seemed to him that he had tramped miles before he spotted a familiar landmark on the northern skyline, yet his mind was less interested in that fact than in locating his mule. Altogether, examining his chances now, he didn't give much for the likelihood of his running across the beast — even if his enemies had not earlier claimed it and its load for their own — and it was, therefore, something of a shock when he came upon it in the ordinary course of his walking. The mule had found itself a pleasant meadow to graze near the waterside, and it stood not fifty yards away from the marshal's route up country.

The animal gave Haggard no trouble to catch and, after leading it out of sight behind a spiky thicket of buckthorn, he untied the sacks containing his supplies and clean garments from its back. Then he made a change of clothing, and felt far more comfortable when it was done. Next he turned his attention to building a fire and getting some food and hot drink into him. Ravenous, he ate almost all the bread and jerked beef he had available and, no less thirsty, he drank three pints of coffee. The taste and smell of everything was a joy in itself.

Lying on the grass, with the first of the day's sun shining across him, he rested and gave his digestion a chance. He truly felt a new man and started to think in terms of his job and responsibilities again. Had he been armed, he might well have paid another visit to the cave where Black Jo and her gang holed up, but the outlaws had his Winchester and his revolver was lying at the bottom of the Pecos with his dead horse. This being how it was, he would have to forget any new foray against the gang until after he had rearmed himself.

His mind went back now to that curious experience which he had had yesterday evening after climbing out of the river. Had there been somebody watching him from that shadowy stand of timber or had he imagined it? Why should he have felt that strange conviction that Jo Callard was among the tree trunks and both pleased and relieved that he was still alive? The woman had had every reason to want him dead, and had indeed been doing all in her power to bring about his death. It must have been his imagination! He'd had one hell of a day, hadn't he? Everybody knew that a man who had been in a state of deep stress was liable to form false impressions about things on the emotional level, and he had surely been in a state of deep stress.

Yes, once more he had to admit it to himself. For all her crimes, he had been taken with Black Jo, and he believed that she had fancied him. But there again he had been dealing with another fleeting impression that had resulted from a heavily charged situation and it might be wise to discount it entirely now. He would accept, too, that he had imagined the woman's presence in the riverside dusk and dismiss those feelings that he had had for her at the time. It was likely that a buck had trodden on the stick which he had heard snap. Oh, to blazes with it all! Keep it as simple as it really was. It was his job to catch Black Jo, and that was what he was going to do.

With this renewed sense of purpose fixed in his mind, Haggard got to his feet, extinguished his fire with the dregs of his coffee pot, and returned his bags to the back of his mule, leaving room for him to fork the beast and ride it. He was going to journey to the not too far distant town of Sheffield, which stood higher up the river, and make a few inquiries there concerning Jo Callard — for no other reason than that Chris Daggart had suggested that he had once seen her there in one of her periods when she was away from the gang. It was, of course, a hunch of sorts and, while it was not his habit to play hunches, it seemed to him — for all his foregoing good intentions regarding her — that he was linked to the woman in some remarkable way and he would always have the power to find her. Yes, it was weird, and he might be going a touch crazy, but there it was and nothing would change it. On the one hand he was determined to deny a romantic interest in the woman, while on the other he was tacitly acknowledging to himself the kind of link with her that was said to connect only those who belonged to each other by the decree of heaven. Soulmates, as that English writing lady called them in that story of hers about the wild moorlands in that far off Yorkshire from which his ancestors had hailed. But wasn't that another good joke? And on him too! How could the grim, tough, almost too moral Deputy U.S. Marshal Frank Haggard think of being linked by love to a woman who was the devil's own? It was a contradiction of all the elements concerned. It didn't make sense. Which more or less brought him back to where he had started from.

Climbing astride his mule's back and guiding the brute by the sides of its headstall, Haggard rode away from the river and out into the prairie beyond. For a time he had the rockface which housed Black Jo's hideout in sight, and he used the land craftily to make his passage across it less conspicuous, but presently he swung back around the stone formations of the neighbourhood and picked up the line of the river again. He headed directly for Sheffield now, judging it to be between thirty five and forty miles away. Keeping his eyes on the lift — for the possibility of the unexpected happening again was always there in his life — Haggard rode steadily on his slow but enduring mount throughout the whole of the day, though he did take brief rests when he felt he must, and it was into the evening when the dense grasses of the virgin plain started giving way to the kind of chewed-off graze which was the unmistakable mark of the cattle ranges. There were signposts and sections of fence about too, and one of the former — an axe-cut job with the lettering burned rather crudely upon it — informed him that Sheffield was just four miles distant. So, with his ride nearing its end, Haggard admitted to himself that he was once more close to exhaustion and in need of some medical care and attention.

But, with the river flowing placidly on his left — generally full to the banks along here and glistening in the western light — the marshal had yet to bring the town in sight, when a shot banged off a short way up country of him and he glanced round quickly to see two young, lean-bodied men hammering towards him on horseback, one of them brandishing a smoking rifle above his head. Haggard brought his mule to a halt, and eased himself off the bones of its back, wincing. After that, relaxing as much as he could, he sat waiting; for, unarmed, he could hardly put on an aggressive front and realized that he had only the authority of his badge to protect him — if the need should prove to be there. "Hello, boys!" he called jocularly, as the two riders, pink-cheeked, round-eyed, straight-nosed and pretty much alike in all other respects, slowed towards him, reins held high and stirrups stretched. "You got money to burn?"

"What d'you mean?" asked the slightly younger of the pair, the one holding the rifle in fact.

"Shooting off cartridges like that!" Haggard explained. "They're getting mighty expensive these days. Haven't you found?"

"Well, yeah," the fellow with the rifle admitted. "What ain't? A dollar a day don't go far."

"Goes further than nothin'," the older of the pair sniffed. "You've sure got a winner there — marshal."

84

Haggard patted his mule. "He does."

"But a ridin' marshal on a mule!"

"It'd be a sight worse if it was a mule on a riding marshal," Haggard commented, tongue in cheek. "So how are you boys named?"

"Ernest and William Ensan," the older fellow said proudly. "How are you named?"

"John Law."

"Oh, ah! Do I raise my hat?"

"I didn't know they made 'em that big."

"Ain't he a cough drop!"

"Frank Haggard, boys."

"Well, Mr Frank Haggard — sir — the law can trespass too!"

"Well, I guess it can at that, Ernie," Haggard admitted. "It is Ernie?"

The older of the twosome nodded. "That's William."

"You surprise me."

"We're brothers."

"I had kind of figured that," the marshal said. "So I'm trespassing on your land?"

"Ain't our land," the younger Ensan responded waspishly. "These here parts bein' what they are, me'n Ernie ain't likely to get more'n six feet of Boot Hill. You can get planted there, but you sure don't grow. And you sure as heck can't raise cows on that stone heap!"

"What're you worried about, son?" Ernie demanded of his brother. "Come Nineteen-forty, when you get there, they'll likely have done the place with fertiliser. Might grow somethin'."

"I'll be nigh on eighty, y'pig!"

"So you might grow young again," Ernie haw-hawed.

"Who does own this land?" Haggard inquired patiently.

"Tom Burke."

"Once of Clarion Town?"

"How'd you know that, Marshal?"

"I hail from there myself."

"Worse places, I suppose."

"Right on the nose, Ernie."

"Well, I got somethin' right anyhow."

"Where is Tom, boys?"

"You his pal or somethin'?"

"He was my pa's friend once," Haggard explained more seriously. "In that great long-ago, when you weren't and I barely was."

"Hot damn!"

"What's up, Willy?" Haggard asked of the younger Ensan brother.

"It's the boss!" announced Willy, who had been craning for a moment or two past and now pointed northwards at a heavy-set rider who was punishing a roan mare as he galloped towards them.

"You've gone and done it, son!" Ernie chortled. "Old Tom will have the cuttin' knife out to you. They'll have to leave the gettin' of the next generation o' Ensans all to yours truly."

"What the heck was you ever true to, Ernie?" Willy pouted. "You wanna hear what Emily's got to say about you."

"Oh, her!"

"That's a nice way to talk about your intended, I must say."

"If you must say anythin', Willy — shut up!"

The heavily built man on the roan mare arrived a few moments later. He reined in, glowering at Willy Ensan and his Winchester. "Damn your eyes, William!" he bellowed. "I've told you about firing that blasted rifle before! What between starting stampedes and cows dropping calves before due, you've caused more trouble with that weapon than a whole regiment of normal idiots!"

"Sorry, boss," Willy Ensan mumbled. "You did say trespassers gotta be stopped."

"Trespassers," Burke almost sobbed, turning his faded blue eyes heavenwards and causing his bushy moustache to bristle under the broad nostrils of his weathered nose. "Trespassers, by God! Don't I have the Ensan boys for my sins?"

"But we got a trespasser!" Willy implored. "Can't y'see, Tom?"

Burke turned his wrathful glare on

to Haggard, who raised a finger and smiled. "Hi, Tom," he greeted.

The man on horseback studied the marshal for a long moment. "Frank?" he asked uncertainly, bringing himself back under control and starting to see beyond his previous anger. "Young Frank?"

"Frank — yes, Tom," Haggard acknowledged. "Though not so young any more."

"Lawman, eh?" Burke mused. "I heard you'd joined Judge Bracknell's riding marshals."

"We're Federal men, Tom," Haggard said. "The judge is our supervisor, as you might say."

"What are you doing in this neck-of-the-woods, Frank?"

"My job."

"I should mind my own business," Burke agreed. "That mule! Tut, tut. You look bad, Frank."

"I've felt better," Haggard admitted.

"That's a nasty place on your neck. Bullet wound, isn't it?"

"Yes."

"Your wrists and hands look raw. Burns?"

"Uh, huh."

"You need a doctor."

"I have it in mind to visit the sawbones in Sheffield."

"You're coming home with me, Frank," Burke said in tones that brooked no argument. "I'll send for the doctor. Right now. William, ride into Sheffield and ask Doc Hordle if he'll come out to the Broken B."

"I can make it into town, Tom." Haggard assured the other. "I'm still functional, and I don't feel greatly amiss. I wouldn't doubt your doctor's a busy man."

"Neither would I," Burke admitted. "But it isn't so far out to my place, and I owe your late father something. It was his money put me in my first business. Today his son plainly needs a little help and hospitality. It's my privilege to offer it. If ever a man looked as if he could do with a few

90

"You'll be thirty-five now."

"Thirty-six."

"Plenty old enough to know your own mind."

"And then some."

"No woman in your life?"

"Not that you'd notice," Haggard replied dismissively. "So you're ranching these days. How's it going?"

A shadow crossed Burke's large face, with its numerous seams and sandy wrinkles, and he drew up his right shoulder and let it settle again. "So-so."

"Only that? What's the trouble?"

"Circumstances," the rancher returned, his manner now off-hand.

"Sure," Haggard conceded, "it's my turn to mind my own business."

"I don't know," Burke said rather heavily and deliberately — "I don't know. It could be your business."

"Rustlers, maybe?"

"Among other things."

"When were they not?" Haggard questioned, his sympathy emerging as a sigh. "You've got it, and they don't see why you should have it. It's a bad old world, Tom."

"You'd know, Frank."

"Better than most," Haggard agreed, waiting for his companion to add something more illuminating; but the foregoing talk seemed to have had a depressing effect on the cattleman and he became abruptly silent and withdrawn. The marshal was slightly nonplussed, but then he remembered that Tom Burke had always tended to be like that — even to the point of the characteristic having been generally remarked — and that as a rule it meant only that the man had found something of true importance to think upon that he didn't wish, or perhaps feel able, to speak about.

The silence remained between them as they rode on. Then, within the next minute or two, the land tilted a trifle downhill and a ranch site became visible at the lowest spot. Built mostly of local stone, a new house stood four-square

the family anyway," Burke responded lightly, entering into the spirit of it all. "He's wearing a badge almost as big as Texas on his shirt, but he doesn't appear to have a gun between him and the poorhouse."

"Circumstances," Haggard confided.

"A touch," the rancher allowed. "A touch and no mistake!"

"If you want to be a real help, Tom — " the marshal began.

But then a rifle spoke from a point too far away to the left of the ranch yard, and Burke clutched at his body and spun round twice under the force of the bullet's impact, falling heavily.

In that instant Haggard could do no more than gape. This business of 'circumstances' had ceased to be a joke.

5

AVOIDING more than one glance at the shocked and frightened Sally, the marshal dropped to his knees and carefully rolled Tom Burke on to his back. Haggard saw at once that the rancher had been hit just below the outer part of his left shoulder and was still very much alive though barely conscious. "Look after him, Sally!" he ordered, and jerked the revolver out of Burke's holster. Then thrusting the weapon into the top of his own trousers, he sprang up again and freed the cattleman's horse from the hitching rail adjacent.

Turning the big mare to face up country, Haggard swung into the saddle and kicked the horse into motion. He crossed the ranch yard like an avenging fury and, leaving it through a line of birch trees, fetched the rancher's mount

blood was starting to seep from his mouth.

Haggard rode right up to the shot badman. Swinging down, he made a quick examination of the inert figure. Padman had received a bullet in the heart and would never breathe again. Nodding his satisfaction, Haggard promptly remounted and rode back to the ranch yard, where he saw that Sally Burke had got her father to his feet and was now doing her best to support him into the house. But Tom Burke was a heavy man, and the girl obviously needed all the help she could get; so, arriving at the kitchen door, Haggard reined back and jumped down, catching the rancher around the waist and steadying him indoors.

"Let's get him upstairs," Sally gasped.

"No," Tom Burke said. "Put me in the chair beside the hearth."

The girl pointed to the right. Haggard steered the wounded man across the kitchen floor. Then the pair were able to unite their strength and lower the rancher into the chair of which he had spoken. "Thank you," Burke whispered, his eyes shut and his face strained and bloodless. "There's an irony in this, Frank."

"How so?"

"I sent for the doctor, boy — for you."

"That you did," Haggard acknowledged. "Well, there's work for him now all right."

"Where's my gun?"

"I have it here," the marshal said. "May I keep it for now, Tom? I need to borrow it."

"Take it as a gift, Frank. My holster too."

"Just a borrow," Haggard insisted.

"You — you went after the — the varmint, didn't you?"

"Yes."

"Did you catch him?"

"I killed him, Tom."

Sally Burke gave a gasp of horror. "Oh, Frank!"

"It's no good, Sally," Haggard said

remarked. "They held up the Fort Standish stage yesterday, and the word's out they did pretty well for themselves." He swallowed dryly. "Why would a member of that gang want to shoot me?"

"Come now, Tom," Haggard said shortly, "you must have a better idea of that than I. Guys like Padman don't as a rule have reasons. They're hired. Set on. Paid killers. I'm asking who'd be likely to pay to have you bushwhacked. And I'd like to know why. Even if you've only some idea — and I daresay I could just about swallow that — do us both a favour and speak it."

Tom Burke kept his eyes sealed and gave his head a small but emphatic shake. It was obvious from his expression that he knew things the law should know, but he wasn't going to talk.

"Dammit, Tom," the marshal exploded. "How can I help you if you won't help me? This has been coming up from the start. There was all that palaver about trespassers on your range. Well, what the hell! Every spread has its trespassers. There are still saddletramps who can't abide bobwire and such."

"That's enough, Frank!" Sally snapped. "You leave him alone. He's afraid of more trouble."

"How much more can he have?" Haggard demanded. "A man has tried to kill him. There's got to be pure hate behind that. A guy with that kind of hate gnawing in his guts doesn't stop at one failure. There are times, Sally, when by trying to avoid trouble you only make more of it."

"I'm not a fool!" the girl protested. "I know that's true!"

"Then you do the talking."

"No, Sally!" her father warned.

"Sally," Haggard urged.

"No," the girl said, lowering her eyes from the lawman's face and turning her back on him. "I have to respect my father's wishes. I'm not sure that unburdening to you would protect dad." She gnawed at

and the boss be wantin' anything more afore I cut off home?"

"Go," Sally said.

"Not so fast, young man," Haggard said authoritatively. "I've got a job for you. There's a dead man lying out on the grass. I want you to help me get him into the barn."

Ernie looked woebegone. "Don't know as I want — "

"Do as you're told!" Tom Burke barked at him, coughing slightly from the effort. "Get the buckboard out. The marshal can use it to take the remains into town — when he gets round it."

"Tomorrow will be soon enough," Haggard confirmed. "You can't do much for a dead man — except bury him — and I don't figure Padman will have many relatives and friends at his funeral." He took a deep breath, and the recently formed scab on his neck wound stretched enough to sting. "Come on, tinribs! The sooner the job's done, the sooner you get off home."

"Ernest!" Burke called seriously.

"Mr Burke?"

"I've a suspicion the marshal may start asking you questions. Be careful what you say. Because you don't know anything, do you?"

"What about?" Ernie Ensan asked vacuously.

"Anything at all!"

Ensan scratched his head. "Well, you're always tellin' me I'm plain ignorant. Anything, hey?"

"Anything at all!" the rancher repeated.

The young man raised a finger in salute and turned away from the door, vanishing into the yard. Haggard walked out of the kitchen behind him, mouth compressed, for he wasn't best pleased by what he had just heard. Even friends could go too far, and the law could be obstructed. But that would keep for now. He and Ernie Ensan had a necessary job to do, and neither of them was too keen on it.

They arrived at the barn. Gesturing

the opposite end of the ranch yard, but he had yet to reach the brute when two other men came riding into the empty space. One of them was Willy, the younger Ensan brother, while the second was a much older man, lean and elegant, with piercing black eyes, an aquiline nose, a thin but shapely mouth, and silver tips beneath the sides of his black Spanish hat. Expensively tailored, to match the rest of his superior presence — and with a medical bag hooked to his pommel — there could be no doubt that this man was Doctor Hordle.

Haggard held back. He watched while a few words were exchanged at the further end of the yard, then saw the Ensan boys depart in the direction of town. But the doctor came slowly on and, halting at the hitching rail outside Tom Burke's back door, dismounted, fetching down his medical bag with him. He was met by Sally in that moment, and she beckoned him into the kitchen, speaking a string of quick words which the watcher's ear could not quite catch. After that Haggard started forward again, and a few moments later he, too, went indoors — noting at once, as he glimpsed the figures receding through a door at the back of the room, that Tom Burke was being helped into the front of the house and presumably to bed; so, reckoning that his added presence could only be a nuisance, he went to the wooden armchair that the rancher had previously occupied and sank tiredly into it, telling himself that he would be quite happy to wait for attention until such time as Burke had been fixed up and Sally or her father remembered that he was there and told Doctor Hordle about him. Thus it was that he yawned cavernously and then fell asleep. A hand shook him awake what he knew from the state of the light must be a good while later. Startled, he blinked upwards and saw Sally Burke bending over him, while behind her stood the doctor's tall shape. "Sorry you've been left alone for so long," the

freight yard tomorrow."

"The dead have the right to some respect," Doctor Hordle observed, "The undertaker's shop is the best place for a corpse."

"If that's what you want," Haggard said indifferently.

"I don't want," the medico responded, a faint edge to his voice. "I simply have the wish to see things done properly."

"We'd rather have it off the premises, Frank," Sally said.

"It's settled," the marshal acknowledged. "Thanks, Doc."

"The sheriff will have to know."

"I'll see him tomorrow, Doc. Had planned to anyhow."

Hordle nodded, repacking his medical bag. When the medico had finished, Sally Burke indicated the door and led him out into the yard. Rising from his chair, Haggard sauntered over to the threshold himself and, taking up a leaning stance against the door jamb, watched the pair walk over to the barn. They vanished inside, and perhaps five minutes went by. Then they reappeared, Doctor Hordle driving the buckboard and the girl striding along beside it. They came up to the kitchen door, where the medico halted the vehicle, and Sally freed Hordle's mount from the hitching rail and tied it to the waggon's tail. After that the doctor slapped the reins on his pulling horse and sent the buckboard rolling out on to the grass, where he turned it in the direction that the marshal knew the town of Sheffield must lie. "That's that," Sally said, dusting off her hands and casting an eye around the dusky horizon. "I think it a good job done."

Haggard gave his chin a jerk, feeling privately that it had all been a lot of fuss about nothing, and he stepped away from the door and let the girl re-enter the kitchen. "Frank," she said, "you must be hungry. What would you like to eat?"

"I can wait for breakfast," he answered. "What I need is a good night's sleep."

into an almost immediate sleep.

He might have lain thus until dawn, dreaming pleasantly enough; but he was awakened during the darkest of the dark hours by the heat gathering under the dry dressings which Doctor Hordle had bound over his burns. For a while he lay trying to will back this discomfort, but the heat became an itching also, and before long the very fact of being in bed developed into an added torment for him. He stuck it for a further half an hour; then, expressing his disgruntlement in an angry groan, got up and lighted the lamp again, figuring that he'd feel a lot more comfortable downstairs in that large old kitchen chair; so, pulling on his garments as a matter of decency, he quietly left his bedroom, lamp in hand, and made his way down into the hall and then through into the kitchen, where he set his light upon the table.

Jaws rubbering frequently over his muttered curses, since he was still dog-tired, Haggard headed for the wooden armchair beside the hearth, but had yet to lower himself into it, when the window at the further end of the room suddenly dissolved into fragments of glass and a fair sized missile came hurtling inwards and fell just short of the kitchen table.

Badly startled, Haggard gazed rather stupidly at the object which had burst in upon him — seeing that it looked like a bundle of short but thick sticks which had been tied together with a piece of string — but it occurred to him in the same instant that sparks were spluttering from the nearer end of it and that he could smell gunpowder burning. Hair bristling on his nape, the marshal realized that he was staring at a homemade bomb and that detonation of the same could only be moments away.

the left of the front door, believing that this was where the new threat lay; and, though he knew that retreat would be much the wiser course, he allowed his impetus to carry him to the middle of the suspect room in the knowledge that he had probably passed a point of no return, and that if a bundle of dynamite the size of the one that he had just rendered harmless should now go off, the front of the house might well collapse and bury him under the debris. He dared not think just then of his almost suicidal rashness. He was there, and that was that.

The dynamite was there. The bundle appeared to have hit a table in the centre of the floor and bounced off on to the carpet in front of the fireplace. Setting his lamp aside once more, Haggard pounced on the second bomb and yanked out its fuse also, praying to God that this time he had come to the end of it. But his prayer was not answered. For he heard a third window shatter — this one in the room on the other side of the hall — and not daring now to even pause for long enough to snatch up his lamp again, he erupted from the room which he had just made safe and went headlong at the partially open door opposite. This was dimly illuminated by the light shining out of the entrance through which he had just projected himself, and the woodwork swung quickly and crashed against the wall on the right as he struck it, admitting him to the room beyond at a pace that beggared description.

Haggard caught himself in mid-stride. He looked around him wildly, seeing the red reflection of a third fuse trembling on the ceiling towards the further end of the room in which he now stood. He tried to place the source of the glow, attempting also to think clearly, but the darkness was a form of confusion in itself. He wallowed in its clinging presence, doing all in his power to spot where the bomb was lying and likewise to shake off the numbing paralysis which had abruptly rooted him. He sweated over his maddening inability to act, but then, reaching the pitch of desperation, he gave a terrific mental heave and broke his inertia, moving forward again in sensible disregard for the uncertainty of his goal.

Ataxic to a degree, the marshal lurched into the further part of the room, darting frantic glances this way and that, and suddenly he smelled burning other than that which had to do with the chemical compounds on the fuse. Indeed, the odour was that of smouldering animal hair and, following the stench with his nose, he saw the bundle of dynamite he sought lying on the part of the bearskin rug that had become trapped under the front legs of a couch.

Kneeling, Haggard whipped the bomb into his grasp, then peered at the fuse. It had burned down far shorter than had the other two, and the fire was ready to enter the tamping. He plucked at it swiftly with finger and thumb, but it was too late for that. The flame was still visible, yes, but the fuse above its point of attachment to the sticks of high explosive had dissolved. Nothing could prevent the detonation now, short of the bomb's instant immersion in a bucket of water, and Haggard reacted instinctively once more, hurling the dynamite from him with all his strength. The bomb ripped through the window, close to the spot at which it had originally smashed into the room, and flew on for perhaps a dozen yards more, abruptly tearing itself apart in a vivid scarlet flash and giving out a thunderous roar that seemed to split the marshal's eardrums. Next moment what was left of the window appeared to burst inwards and debris streamed at and about him, an enormous concussion hurling him backwards and to the floor, where he lay barely conscious and praying anew that this effort to destroy the Broken B ranch house had now been completed, since he knew himself spun out and incapable of countering any further effort to blow the place apart.

This time, however, as the moments passed and no new sounds of violence reached him, it did seem to be done with and, when a full minute had gone by and he felt able to scramble up again, he knew for certain that the threat was over and he had saved the house, at least for now.

A light approached him, and he began shakily to brush himself down, conscious of much dust and many tiny bits of glass and wood clinging to his garments. Blinking through the radiance of the lamp, as it halted about a yard from him, Haggard made out a pale faced Sally Burke looking at him with a pair of big eyes in which he saw a kind of questioning bewilderment that stabbed his badly jangled nerves to anger. "Well, what d'you think you're seeing?" he demanded, as if she were accusing him of being wilfully to blame for all the damage that had just occurred.

"What — what's happened, Frank?"

Haggard told her exactly. He started with how he had come to get up, went on to how he had entered the kitchen within moments of the dynamite arriving there, told then of how he had also snuffed out the first of the bombs at the front of the house and been just short of doing the same with the second, and concluded: "You're mighty fortunate to have a home left, Sally, and the three of us in the house are lucky to still be alive!"

"Oh, Frank!" the girl exclaimed. "I — I just didn't know. This — this is all getting too much!"

"Too much?" Haggard inquired rather brutally.

"Of what? Who for? Blast it! I warned you, didn't I? It's clear to me, even as an outsider, that — "

"We don't need your wretched warnings!" Sally Burke retaliated, angry herself now. "You always did believe yourself twice as smart as the rest of us put together, Frank Haggard!"

"How about you tell me what you and your dad are up to your necks in?" the marshal snapped.

"It's not us!" Sally declared, obviously outraged.

"We haven't done anything!"

"I didn't suppose you had!" he retorted, realizing that much of what was being said was the result of upset nerves and no more than partially reflected what the minds behind the words really intended to say.

"It has to do with the Hamilton Chine Cattle Company," the girl said in a quieter and more reasoned tone, the information nevertheless seeming to be compelled from her by an inner force that she could no longer control. "Chine wants us off this ranch. He wants the land for himself." The oil-lamp shook momentarily in her hand. "Dad owes a heap of money, Frank. We have big debts."

"You folk owe this Hamilton Chine?"

"No," Sally replied. "Let's get this straight. Dad owes a packet to the

129

Everton Moneylenders, who do business in San Antonio. Chine found out long since that we owed them. But it isn't them. They're okay — so long as we keep paying the interest on their loan. It's what that Chine has been trying to stop. Up to now, the whole thing has simply been underhand and the doings real sly and subtle; but now Hamilton Chine seems to have run out of patience. I think he's taken his gloves off and wants to finish us off by any method at all — no matter how terrible." She compressed her lips and shook her head, frowning dismally. "You wouldn't believe!"

"I would," Haggard said. "It all married up with what I know so far. There's a lot of monkey business in Texas these days, and you've a share of greedy people on the river Pecos, Sally."

They both glanced upwards as they heard movements echoing through the ceiling above them.

"That's dad," the girl sighed. "He's

130

trying to get up. He'll never manage it."

"Okay," the marshal said. "You'd better go up there and stop him. Let him know what's happened. He must be feeling groggy after having that slug cut out of him. We can do without the risk of him falling all over the place."

"Can't we just!" Sally agreed fervently; and she left the room without another word, her tread accelerating step by step.

Haggard heard the girl hurry up the stairs and enter her father's bedroom. Irritated words passed briefly between the pair; then what was clearly going to be a longer and quieter conversation got started. Sensing that he could have no part in what the father and daughter wished to say to each other at this time, Haggard left the now almost total darkness of the damaged room and re-entered the hall — crossing it to step through into the place where he had left his light. Then, lamp in hand, he went back upstairs and returned to his room, where he once more climbed into bed — sitting with his back to its headrail now and dozing — and there he stayed with hardly a movement until the dawn paled into the east and he heard Sally rise again, look first into her father's room, and then go downstairs, clearly with a view to beginning the new day in earnest.

After giving the girl half an hour to herself — for she was the mistress of the house and probably had a list of early morning duties that she preferred to see through on her own — Haggard got up also and went down to the kitchen, where he was immediately offered a mug of hot black coffee. Nodding his thanks, he asked Sally how she had found her father that morning.

"Sore," she answered, "but otherwise himself."

"Does he know about the things you told me last night?"

"Of course. I told him the first chance I got."

"It's okay?"

"It's done."

"I've done some thinking," Haggard said deliberately, "and I've made up my mind that I'm going to look into your troubles before I leave the district. I figure the attempt that Ike Padman made to bushwhack your father gives me all the excuse I need. Black Jo Callard's gang is my business, and Padman was one of Black Jo's men."

"You told us, Frank."

He jerked his chin again. "You spoke to me about a cattle company."

"Hamilton Chine's."

"I gathered dirty tricks had been played on you."

"That's what I'd call poisoning water, feeding cows loco weed, and putting beeves infected with hoof-and-mouth into our herd, wouldn't you?"

Haggard made a face.

"That's without the rustling and such?"

"Such?"

133

"Range butchering for one thing, and a plague of cats for another."

"Just wanted to know all of it," the marshal said.

"This Chine fellow doesn't miss much."

"He's a bag of wind," Sally said contemptuously.

"His wife has the brains."

"She runs things?"

"From the background. Or so people say."

"Happens in the best regulated of families," Haggard commented. "Poison, loco weed, diseases — your animals would have been killed off at graze mainly."

"We were once very prosperous," Sally agreed bitterly. "We employed two dozen men, and our bunkhouse was well spoken of. Now we employ two. You met them yesterday."

Haggard put the heel of his right hand on his brow, and gave his head a shake, grinning at the ceiling. "The Ensans."

"Ernest and William, as dad calls them."

"But you have other names for them?"

"Quite often, Frank," the girl admitted. "If only they could learn to concentrate for more then ten seconds at a time."

"Yet they're honest where it matters?"

"We can trust them in the important things, yes."

"Sally, there's something with everybody," Haggard reminded, completely serious again. "What I don't quite get in all this is why people who want your land would take the risk of ruining it permanently with weed spores and a long-term infection."

"We've been puzzled by that too," the girl admitted. "And the more so because the lie of the district places us well down river and quite separate from the nearest of the cattle company's land. No, dad and I don't see the Box B as a ready part of the Chine empire. So why do they want us so desperately? It's contradictory really, if you look deeply enough into it."

"You convince me of it too," Haggard confessed. "It looks like the cattle company is going to a lot of trouble to hog an expanse of grass they can't really want. As a rule, men will only put themselves out to acquire something that's vitally necessary as part of an obvious plan. Yet here, going on what you say, we seem to have an exception."

"You can rely on me," Sally assured him. "But talk to John Sell about it. You intend to meet the sheriff this morning, don't you? John may be able to supply a few ideas I can't."

"We'll see."

"Oh, dad said I was to tell you."

"Tell me what?"

"You can borrow a horse from the corral, and have his gun too."

"Thank you," Haggard said, his gratitude entirely genuine. "That's help of a real kind. My poor old stallion took a bullet and ended up in the river."

"An outlaw bullet?"

"Uh, huh."

"You've obviously been through a rough time recently," the girl observed. "Tell me about it while I get breakfast."

So, seating himself in the wooden armchair that stood on the hearth, he did just that — going into more detail than would usually have been the case, if he had talked at all — and he concluded with the comment that he'd catch up with Black Josephine Callard one of these fine days and give her the same kind of hard ride back to Clarion Town that he had previously given a dozen or so of her male counterparts.

"You said she's beautiful," Sally Burke remarked.

"Did I?" Haggard questioned, surprised at himself. "I reckon bad covers most of it." He glimpsed the knowing expression on the girl's face. "Why shouldn't she be a looker? Anyhow, I reckon she'd be pure dazzling if she dropped that hausfrau lash-up she does her hair in."

"Watch it, Frank!"

"Watch what?"

"My poor late mother always used to say that the Haggard boy had a liking for the wrong kind of women."

"I've never noticed," the marshal responded, a trifle put out. "Fact is, Sally, women haven't figured very largely in my life. Sure, I admire all the fine things about a lovely girl, but I have it all under control."

"I've heard men talk like you before."

"Not me, you haven't."

"Eggs?"

"Please, Sally."

"Fried bread?"

"It's no breakfast without it."

The girl nodded and went on with her work at the stove. In fact she completed her frying without saying another word, though she had the elements of a secret smile at the corners of her mouth and eyes. Then, straightening from her bent position over the skillet, she carried Haggard's food to a place which she had already laid for him at the table and served it deftly enough, transferring her utensils to the sink immediately afterwards. At her gesture, the marshal left the wooden armchair and went over to one of the dining variety, drawing it up to the table and sitting down to eat in the now fragrant atmosphere of the kitchen, while Sally Burke left him and walked through into the front of the house, audibly entering the room which had been damaged by the blast from the dynamite the night before.

Sally re-entered the kitchen just as Haggard had put back the last of his food and was pouring himself another mug of coffee from the pot. "It's a sight through there," she remarked. "I can see several days' work for a builder."

"It could have been a heck of a lot worse," Haggard reminded.

"Yes," the girl agreed. "There could easily have been no house left at all. I found the dynamite that should have gone off in here when I first came down. And the other in the drawing room."

"What did you do with it?"

"I dropped it into the rain butt at the end of the house," she answered, jerking her head to the right.

"As good a place as any," Haggard approved. "It's dangerous stuff to leave lying around, but it can't do any harm in there."

"We owe you so much, Frank," Sally said in a grave but forthright voice. "You most probably saved our lives as well as our home."

"I saved my own skin too," he responded. "Now, Sally, if you'll show me to that horse and tack."

"I'll saddle up for you," Sally said briskly. "Sit there. Give your food a chance to digest."

Haggard raised a finger in acquiescence. He was quite content to let the girl do things as she wished. But, after she had gone out into the yard, he lost all desire to sit around and rose to his feet, leaving the table and passing out of the kitchen into the hall, where he saw that Sally had opened the front door wide and then felt the morning breeze blowing pleasantly through the opening and smelling faintly of the river.

He entered the room where the damage from the single bomb to explode had occurred the night before. It was indeed a mess in there, with lumps of plaster, pieces of glass, dust, and flakes of whitewash all over the floor and furniture. The windowspace — beyond which the explosion had taken place — had been rent jagged. Lengths of the frame hung and jutted from it at all angles, brickwork had been bared at numerous points above and below the sash, and the sill had come away completely and now lay on the floor between its original bedding and the couch against which it had clearly been hurled after the explosion had torn it out of the room's front wall. The marshal studied the ruins, calculating for himself. Yes, Sally had assessed it correctly. It would take several days of skilled labour to put right the damage done here. The impoverished Tom Burke would undoubtedly have to dig deeper into his pocket than he might like.

Haggard stepped back into the hall. Making a right turn, he passed out of the front door. Pausing on the step, he spent a few moments gazing towards the Pecos, then sauntered a short distance forward, looking down at the area of new grass in front of the house where flash marks showed that the explosion had occurred in the air above the ground. He sniffed at the breeze. A faint odour of nitrates still lingered out here, and the memories thus stirred caused Haggard to go hot and cold all over.

He felt strongly now how matter-of-fact and almost irresponsible his behaviour had been after the detonation. He had made no attempt to leave the house and seek the thrower — or throwers — of the dynamite bombs.

That had really been obligatory. It all seemed so peculiar and unreal this morning. Yes, he had his excuses. He had been dazed and shaken up by the blast, and his brief fight with Sally Burke had also taken its toll. Yet, violently concussive as it had all been, he had not been put fully out of action for more than a minute or two and should have given a far better account of himself. Sadly, the whole episode appeared now to occupy his mind in a state of isolation. Only the visible evidence of the blast itself offered proof to him that the explosion had actually taken place. Sally Burke had the local knowledge to guess at its perpetrators, but he had no idea what they looked like. He could well have been bombed by ghosts for what true reality he could find in all of it this morning.

The marshal suddenly stirred uneasily. He glanced up and around, peering intently where white mists, born of the river, spun and wavered among the low humps and sagging ridges that gave the general flatness of the land between him and the Pecos a little character. That sixth sense of his was at work again. He felt a tingling magnetism in his spine, and a faint pulsing above and between his eyes. He was being watched. But from where? And were those spying eyes keeping company with a rifle? Part of his mind implored him to get back indoors, but another part of it advised him to stay calm and keep quartering — because it could be to his advantage.

Letting his gaze sweep slowly around the tight arc of land and sky which was all he had to explore — since the blocking presence of the Broken B ranch house cut off almost every sight to his rear — Haggard saw nothing to excite his attention, and he was nearing the conclusion that this was a morning for untrustworthy states of mind, when he detected a male figure hardening into sight atop a small eminence which was situated well to the right of his middle view.

The man was undoubtedly the watcher who had produced the recent peculiar sensations in Haggard. For he stood considering the marshal with what was obviously a long-focussed stare. Nor did he attempt to drop back out of sight again, when he perceived that he was himself now discovered — for it seemed uncertain as to whether he had actually intended it — though it was also true that he made no immediate effort to communicate. He simply stood there, very broad of shoulder, remarkably square in stance, and tall without being unusually so. His hands were in his pockets, and he had the air about him of one morose and unsure. As if he had, after long consideration, made up his mind on a course of action, only to renounce his decision almost at once and start his cogitations anew. But then he appeared to renew that earlier decision and, relaxing, drew both hands from his pockets and lifted his arms in the air, beckoning with them, in short bursts at first and then with a continuous vigour that left Haggard in no doubt as to what was required of him.

The marshal hesitated for a moment, then started towards the man on the higher ground. He was fairly certain that the other had something for him. It could be information — or, perhaps, a bullet. Well, he had taken enough chances just lately. This was one more to put with the rest.

7

EYES never leaving the figure ahead of him, Haggard moved towards the man's raised position at a good but unvarying pace; and, as he neared the hillock which the other topped, the man himself came down off the low summit and met him, hands once more in his pockets and his seemingly morose aura again apparent. "Good morning," he said in a decently educated voice, his strong, sharply-incised features revealing the odd trace of refinement.

"Morning," Haggard responded, no longer the least bit wary of the stranger as they summed each other up.

"You'll be the U.S. deputy I heard talk of yesterday evening."

"In town?"

"In Sheffield, yes."

"I guess. News travels fast. My name

147

must have come from Doc Hordle."

"Hordle was the source, yes. Him and the sheriff."

"Well, sir, I don't know who you are, but I can tell you that Ike Padman got what he deserved."

"I'd say so. He knew the risks he ran."

"That's fair enough." Haggard nodded grimly. "Who are you?"

"That's not important."

"No? I'd like to know."

"Marshal, it's what I have to tell you that matters, and I feel the need to be quick about it."

"Are you under somebody's eye then?"

"Probably."

"Then I could be too?"

"I expect you know your life's not worth much around here."

Haggard chuckled cynically. "Nor anywhere else. I don't let it worry me."

"I'd say not," the stranger confided. "You look a hard bastard to me."

"Good description."

"So — to business," the other said briskly. "The cattle company is trying to go too fast now. That's why I'm pulling out. If you want to find out what their expansionist plans are all about, take a look at what they're doing over at Rockford Bend. That's the key to it all. Along with the herd they bought up cheap near Carlsbad." He paused, chest arched and tense. "As for Tom Burke and that daughter of his —"

"What about them?"

"What with one thing and another, Marshal, that pair will never know how lucky they are to still be alive," the stranger responded. "Tell them to sell up this very day. Take whatever they can carry and get out. Start again some place far from this. If Carmilla Chine and her husband pull off what I think they're aiming for — and the power is with them — the Broken B will be of no further use to Tom Burke and young Sally."

"I'll carry your message to them, mister," Haggard said, frowning as he pulled thoughtfully at an ear lobe, "but I don't figure they'll see much that's new in it or be a whole lot influenced. No, sir! Not from what I already know about it anyhow. Though I may not be as well informed as I think, and my knowledge could be full of holes."

"Nothing's that complicated, Marshal."

"I've never found it so," Haggard allowed. "Cut through the rind, eh, and the fruit comes spilling out all over the auction?"

The stranger gave his head an emphatic toss, then turned away and started climbing back towards the crest of the low summit on which the marshal had first spotted him. "I'll leave it to you," he said across his shoulder — "damn fool that I am for taking it this far."

"You've told me nothing really!" Haggard protested.

"I've told you everything you need to know," the other retorted, craning

150

momentarily — "and maybe signed my own death warrant to boot!"

Haggard watched the stranger enter the last step or two of his ascent. The man's back was now set squarely to the marshal. It was plain that he did not mean to speak again. The lawman was baffled. Unarmed, he couldn't kick up too much of a fuss about this, as he saw it, somewhat cavalier treatment. Not too many people regarded a Federal badge as the symbol of God Almighty. Nor did he particularly wish to further delay a man who too plainly saw himself as being in some danger of his life. If the stranger said that he had told the law everything that really mattered, then there could be little doubt that he had. The fellow was a fairly superior being, and it was no less certain that he would be entirely sure of what he wished to put over. Better leave it at that. Yet — !

Haggard didn't feel that he could let his rather enigmatic informant get away with it as easily as all that. No, dammit! Even the best had to be made to respect their obligation to the law. "Hey!" he shouted sternly, and went scrambling swiftly towards the top of the mound which the stranger had just crossed, hoping to catch up with the man on the reverse slope; but, by the time he reached the crest, the stranger had already arrived at the bottom of the mound's further side and mounted a horse waiting there. Even as Haggard watched, the fellow put spurs to hide and went galloping off. Nonplussed as he had been, the marshal threw up his hands and shook his head, giving up hope of any additional talk with the departing man and facing about again, his gaze immediately travelling back to the Broken B ranch house, where he saw Sally Burke standing on the front step, everything about her questioning and a gunbelt dangling from her right hand.

Moving off the hillock at a checked run, Haggard hurried back to the house and halted in front of the girl. "Did you see that guy?" he panted.

"Yes."

"Know him?"

"Eli Rumfit. He's the range manager with the Chine cattle company."

"Ah!" Haggard mused, for the man's work clearly fitted with what he had had to tell. "Well, he was the range manager. It seems he's packed it in. He also asked me to bring you and your father some advice."

"What's that, Frank?"

"Sell up and get out of here this very day. He says, when the cattle company has finished its plan for growth, this ranch will be of no use to you and your father." Taking a deep breath, Haggard exhaled hard through lips that he had shaped into an O. "He sees Hamilton Chine and those cattle people as winners, I guess."

"We'll see Mr Rumfit, Hamilton Chine, and all the rest of them, in hell first!"

"Don't doubt," Haggard said. "Well, I've done my part." And he went on to tell the girl the rest of what Eli Rumfit had had to say, finally asking: "Where's Rockford Bend?"

"Up the river," Sally answered. "A mile or two above town. It's just a bend in the Pecos."

"Anything special about it?"

"Not that I'm aware of."

"I did mention that Rumfit said the cattle company is bringing in a herd that it bought over in New Mexico?"

"Yes — from Carlsbad. I don't see any special significance in that either, Frank. A business the size of Chine's depends as much on buying in as it does selling."

"Does the company ever get it wrong?" Haggard believed he'd rephrase that one. "Has the company ever got it wrong?"

Sally hesitated, absently handing Haggard the gunbelt that she had been holding, and he latched it about his waist, muttering a word of thanks as he waited. "We're of the opinion that it did make a serious mistake last year."

"A business mistake?"

The girl inclined her head.

"Tell me about it, Sally."

"Hamilton Chine bought several thousand acres of what we regard as worthless graze to the northwest of our ranch and beyond. It's pretty well waterless."

"I see. What's the extent of their grass reserves? Any idea?"

"It can't be large, Frank." Sally said thoughtfully. "The company didn't send a whole lot of beef to the spring sales. Chine has always seen the fall — with the winter coming up and much heavier killing in the slaughterhouses — as giving the better return on capital outlay. It can pay to hold on to your steers earlier in the year and fatten them up across the summer months."

"Is there any chance that new herd could be bound for the dry grass?"

"You know better than that!" Sally declared shortly. "You were brought up among cattle, Frank. Only a fool

155

would turn a herd that had just been driven hundreds of miles on to dry grass. Water is essential to dehydrated bovines. And you can't fatten anything without it."

"Yet if a dry range is all you have available — ?"

"Provided there was *some* water," the girl stressed, temporising — "possibly. But — Really Frank! Isn't all this speculation? What are you driving at?"

Townwards of them a gun roared, a long, cracking roll to its echo, and Haggard stiffened and chilled, wondering if a man had just died — and whether he knew the man and had been talking to him only a short while ago. He told himself that the very thought was nonsense, but the West was still among the most violent and vengeful places on earth — and when the pattern was there and the shot just about on cue, a man in the know had good cause to fear. "Oh, sure," he said, restoring to Sally what he intended to seem like his guileless attention. "I was only speculating. It's the better part of my job." He paused. "It's time I rode into town. Okay?"

"Your horse is ready and waiting at the hitching rail."

"Good work, Sally," he said warmly, making to step past her.

But she brought down a staying hand into the crook of his left elbow and said: "Don't try to deceive me, Frank. I heard that shot too."

"So did lots more folk," Haggard said. "Ten to one, somebody just bowled over a jackrabbit."

The hand on his arm shook angrily. "You're going to see, aren't you?"

Haggard gave her a curt little nod, and the girl removed her hand from inside his elbow. She gestured for him to walk on, and he passed indoors and on through into the ranch yard. There he found a sorrel stallion waiting for him at the hitching rail. Freeing the beast, he swung up, then spurred off to his right, guiding the horse around the northern end of the house and out into the range beyond, where he headed for the raised ground under which he and Eli Rumfit had earlier spoken together.

Crossing the intervening grass at high speed, he sailed over the hillock and down its further side, peering now across rolling stretches of pasture where the first shadows of the day were marking the place of the newly rising sun. Up river of him, a lingering shade of night was thinning back to reveal rooftops, a church spire, and the smoke curling upwards from a variety of chimneys. The town before him — which was situated mainly on the opposite bank of the Pecos — was unquestionably Sheffield, and not too far ahead of him he made out the sandbanks and pebble-ridged shallows of the ford which linked the range on this side of the river with the built-up area on the other.

A tiny movement caught at the tail of Haggard's left eye. He moved closer to the water, where a thicket of cottonwoods, osiers, and berry bushes edged much of the bank. Now, through the broad green leaves of the hanging boughs, he glimpsed the presence of a riderless horse that was cropping the rich grass at the water's-edge. The sight made him virtually certain that the worst had happened, and within moments he detected a shape doubled up among the tussocks nearer to his old course.

Correcting his line of travel again, the marshal bore down upon the figure lying there. It was Eli Rumfit all right. Deeply concerned, Haggard raised up in his saddle and swung his right leg over the pommel, springing down then from a mount that he had not fully checked, and he came to rest quite close to Rumfit, while his horse trotted ahead for several yards before veering off to the right and stopping, its jaws, too, falling at once to the graze.

Haggard dropped into a kneeling position beside the ex-range manager. There was blood in the grass near

Rumfit's right armpit, and he spotted a bullet-wound in the top of the pectoral muscle on that side. The marshal had expected to find the other dead but, as he bent towards the bleeding man and turned him off his hip and onto his back, Rumfit opened an eye which was still bright with life and hissed: "Watch yourself, Marshal! They're still present!"

"Is that a fact?" Haggard gulped, and he looked sharply up and around, movement at the further end of the riverside thicket seeming to freeze his bowels and bring an electric tremble to his hands. "I see them!"

"Get into cover, man!" Rumfit urged.

Haggard needed no second telling. Five horsemen had emerged from the thicket. They were already well into the open and spurring straight at him. The marshal looked swiftly to his left. The waterside thicket was the only cover around. He had better reach it at the double. If those characters on horseback managed to surround him, he'd be dead before he knew it. Even if his legs weren't the youngest around, it was time to get the lead out!

The marshal straightened his lower limbs. Off he went towards the river at a crouched run. Gunfire crackled in the morning cool. A bullet flicked the slack of Haggard's shirt, and another thudded into the ground just in front of him. Veering slightly, the lawman fairly raced for the vegetation, compensating into a zag to match the zig, but nothing he did threw the hard-riding gunmen off target by much. One slug after another passed, close enough to set his flesh shrinking, and his nape crept and shocks ran up and down his spine in time to the thudding of his soles.

It was touch and go, yet somehow he survived to reach the thicket. Into the heart of the growth he dived, kicking and clawing a way through the thorns and brambles until he emerged among the trees beyond. Here he spun around one of the thickest cottonwoods present and came to a stand at its back, pulling his revolver as he dashed the sweat out his eyes and caught hard at the deepest breath he could manage, holding it until his mind cleared and his nerves steadied.

Yanking round, the riders pounded towards his cover. They were now little more than forty yards away, and he could see their faces clearly. Yes, he had been almost certain of it from the start. The men were the surviving members of Black Jo Callard's gang. They were Chris Daggart, Dan Ward, the small-featured Dilks, Abel Toms and Lance Cowper. He guessed that they were working for the Hamilton Chine Company as a body now, and it figured that they had been sent out that morning to keep an eye on the departing Eli Rumfit. They must have seen the lawman's meeting with the man, expected his traitorous revelations, and drygulched him accordingly. They would have been lying in ambush for Haggard ever since, working on the expectation that their shot at the ex-range manager would bring the marshal to them as a matter of course. It all formed a perfectly logical sequence, and there was no evil sleight of hand present. Yet it was nevertheless remarkable how the gangsters — apparently at a loose end with their boss about to leave them for a spell — had come by such immediate employment with a classy outfit like Hamilton Chine's cattle company. This fact alone seemed to prove that there were still things present that Haggard could not even guess at as yet.

The approaching horses shied back from the thicket. Their riders shouted and swore at them but they had more sense than to breast into the thorns and otherwise entangling brambles. Guns roared, and bullets slammed into the tree behind which Haggard was standing. The shots were an expression of impotence really, since the cottonwood could absorb all the lead the badmen could throw at it and show little sign of damage. The marshal had only to keep himself fully hidden and the shooting would constitute no threat to him worth the mention. But that was obvious, and Haggard knew that the outlaws had sense enough to see it for themselves. And this proved the case a moment later when Chris Daggart bawled: "Let's take the polecat from the downriver end of this tangle! If he retreats in there, he'll only put himself in a worse mess! It gets thicker upstream! He don't know it yet, boys, but he's damn nigh bottled himself in there!"

"Aye, come on!" Dan Ward yelled. "I won't be happy again till I've had my reckonin' with that son-of-a-bitch!"

Haggard smiled sardonically at the words. He hadn't forgotten the lovelorn Ward either. The big man should have his chance when the opportunity arose. But Haggard saw a greater advantage in the moment. His enemies were already riding away from him to the right. All five men — making due allowances for the sometimes intervening trees — were open targets to him just now, whereas they would have to twist round in their saddles to answer any shots from him. The chances of their obtaining a hit were small, but his own were obviously good; so he stepped away from the bole that sheltered him and triggered off the entire contents of his cylinder at high speed. Cowper lifted up and lurched forward in his saddle, badly wounded for a certainty, and Dilks yelled with pain, the capping muscle of his right shoulder largely shot away. Clearly as much enraged by the fact that his Stetson had been shot off as the hurts to his comrades, Daggart reined in and called for answering fire, but Haggard had to do no more than step back into cover and begin a reload while another storm of lead spent itself against the trunk of his cottonwood.

His weapon ready to use again, Haggard peered around the side of his cover, seeking a bonus if the opportunity to earn it were still there;

but he saw that his enemies had already spread out and moved on somewhat, reducing his hope of more fast but effective shooting, and he judged that the outlaws were now pressing on with their original plan and preparing to come in at him from the southern end of the thicket. He realized that bravery and surprise were his two best weapons here, and was preparing to create another piece of startlement for his foes — by going forward to meet them where they might have expected him to stay back — when a pair of rifles interrupted the proceedings with a series of sharp bangs from somewhere to the east of the river. Whether or not there were more hits among the badmen Haggard could not tell from where he stood, but the effect of this unexpected intervention by the unknown riflemen was nothing short of dramatic, for Daggart first uttered a cry of fear and then yelled: "Let's get the out of this, boys! We ain't no duck shoot for the river men!"

Further shots rang out and, while the echoes were flying, the riders must have fetched their mounts about, for they came streaming back across the front of the thicket, momentary targets that Haggard was still too surprised to accept, and went galloping off up the riverside, the sound of their departure quite soon lost upon the deep soil that edged the Pecos here. Silently whistling his relief and giving his brow the further benefit of his sleeve, the marshal tipped his gun back into its holster and found a way out of the thicket which avoided any more damage to his already scratched skin and clothing. Then, standing with the river and the vegetation behind him, he looked eastwards across the land for his saviours and saw familiar figures rise from behind another of those small mounds in the land and stand with rifles slanted over their shoulders as they picked out his shape against the greenery, pointed, and then began to jabber between themselves, nid-nodding frequently in the profundity of their observations.

Sighing to himself anew, Haggard began walking towards them, using his longest strides, while they started sauntering in his direction, come day go day style. "Good morning, Ernie," he said, when the gap between him and the Ensan brothers had narrowed to a few yards — "good morning, Willie."

"There y'are, Ernie," Willy said disgustedly, passing the back of his left hand under his nose, "ain't we gone and started the day just right! Damned if it ain't that long marshal's hide we just went and saved!"

"Well, don't sound quite so happy about it!" Haggard pleaded. "Good souls like you two would have been sure to put flowers on my grave! Heck, boys, you're both old enough by now to know better than to mix yourselves in other people's fights!"

"If only we'd known it was you," Ernie said brazenly. "Comes of our havin' such good eyes."

"Oh?" the marshal said inquiringly, not quite perceiving the drift of that one.

"That's old Jasper yonder, d'you see, sir?" Ernie explained.

"Old Jasper?"

"That there red stud. Miss Sally's horse."

Now Haggard jerked his head comprehendingly. "You boys figured you were fighting for Miss Sally?"

"Her horse," Willy agreed. "It's a wonder old Jasper didn't set about them villains for himself. He sure is a fightin' hoss when his blood's up!"

"He'd have been in there hooves flyin' if it had been Miss Sally," Ernie confided to his brother.

"We ought to've known. That hoss don't care for the law no more'n we do."

"This makes me so sad," Haggard said, grinning all over his face.

"Humph!" Ernie complained. "How do you look when you're happy? Some funny folk take up with the law, Willy.

Said so when John Sell got his badge. He was a ten times better cowhand."

"Aw, what's the use!" Willy sniffed. "We'd better get to work. We're already late, boy. That's docked pay for sure."

"Tom knows you're too rich already," Ernie said disconsolately, facing about and pointing the way back to the mound from which they had recently done their shooting — and which, presumably, was hiding their horses from the marshal's sight. "Move yourself, my man!"

The two young men began trudging away, the prospect of another day's work clearly not altogether to their taste.

"Thank you, fellers!" Haggard called after them.

"You're welcome, suh," Ernie threw back grudgingly.

"See you around."

"Not if we see you first," Willy promised. "Don't get yourself killed now." But the possibility seemed to cheer the younger Ensan no end, for he screwed his head round and revealed an ugly face that wore a beatific smile. "Not unless we can watch!"

Haggard chuckled to himself, then became immensely serious again. It looked like being another of those fraught and very uncertain days; and first off he had a wounded man to get into town. Rumfit had done all right by him, and he wouldn't do less by Rumfit. Somebody was going to pay in full for what that guy was suffering right now.

8

HAGGARD had delivered the wounded Eli Rumfit — borne into Sheffield with some difficulty — to the doctor's surgery and had been assured that the ex-range manager was harder than teak and would be most unlikely to die of the hole drilled in his upper body by a thirty-thirty slug earlier that morning. Now — poised at the head of the main street, where Doctor Hordle had hung out his shingle on a tall, white-walled house — the marshal was looking westwards among the business signs which jutted above the boardwalks and seeking the one that could be expected to indicate the law office. He soon spotted what he sought, on the left and just over half way along the street, and made for the premises at once, leading his borrowed mount and reflecting that, for all the fierce reputation that the Ensan boys had given it, Sally Burke's red horse had so far proved among the most willing and tractable brutes that he had ever ridden.

With the stallion walking at his right shoulder, Haggard arrived outside the law office and, tying the big stud to the hitching rail, lightly brushed himself down with the backs of his still bandaged hands. After that he went into the building, where he saw a six-feet four-inch giant of a man in process of stepping up to the window. The other had a mane of blond hair and the kind of features that made those on a Greek god look second rate.

He now stood looking out at Sally Burke's horse, a tiny frown just touching his wide-set blue eyes.

"Ah, the riding marshal," he observed, without looking at the Federal lawman. "You seem to be a poor relation. Did I hear you're named Haggard?"

173

"Frank Haggard, yes. You're John Sell?"

"I am." Turning to face Haggard now, the sheriff offered a long-fingered hand, and they shook briefly, each summing the other up with a wary smile. "That's Sally Burke's horse."

"So it is, Sheriff," Haggard acknowledged. "And this here is her father's sixgun. There's no telling what else may belong to the Burkes on that horse — but I do still own the seat of my pants."

"That's something, Marshal," Sell allowed.

"What are you doing in Sheffield?"

"Putting my long nose into local affairs."

"I believe it's permitted."

"It is, Sheriff," Haggard said firmly. "Federal means what it says. Not that I intend to tread on your toes more than I must. I've been saddled with the job of bringing in Black Jo Callard and her gang by Judge Bracknell of Clarion Town."

"Or Hang City."

"Eh?"

"That's what it's often called around here these days," the sheriff explained. "Bracknell has a certain reputation, and he's given it to the town."

"Bracknell's severe — and I'm usually his hangman."

"How can you do it, Haggard?"

"Easily — after I've seen what murder looks like."

"You make me feel like a Simon Pure."

"You do one job, Mr Sell, and I do another."

The sheriff pulled a wry jib. "This talk's not going to get us far, is it?"

"No, it isn't," Haggard agreed.

"How can I serve you, Marshal?" Sell inquired. "This isn't just a courtesy call?"

"You know better," Haggard said shortly. "First I'd better tell you. I just put a wounded man by the name of Eli Rumfit into the doctor's surgery. He was drygulched — by guys I know to be the members of Black Jo Callard's gang. The varmints would seem to be working for your local cattle company now. Rumfit had contacted me very early in the day. According to him, Hamilton Chine is up to something at Rockford Bend. The cattle company is bringing in a herd from New Mexico. The two things appear to be related. Do you know anything about it?"

"I know about the herd," Sell replied. "I reckon everybody in town does. A lot of our men work for Hamilton Chine, and there's always some talk. But Rockford Bend — ?"

The sheriff slowly drew up his shoulders and let them settle again. "What the dickens could be going on there? It's just a place on the Pecos."

"That's about what Sally Burke said."

"You've discussed this with Sally?"

"Even to the perplexity she shares with her father concerning all that dry range the cattle company bought," Haggard answered. "I imagine I know most of what there is to know, Sheriff, though I can't say that the Burkes were all that forthcoming to begin with. It wasn't until after the attempt late yesterday to murder Tom that I started getting answers to most of the questions I put. What with one thing and another, Tom Burke has problems — and then some. He and Sally seem to have been getting a real dirty deal from this man Chine and his lot."

"Of whom Eli Rumfit was one of the worst," the sheriff observed. "I don't get him at all."

"It seems he's left the cattle company," Haggard said. "He told me they're in too much of a hurry now. Perhaps he figured on getting while the getting was still good. Though he's shot square with me, I'd say he's a pretty hard case and would never be too scrupulous."

"That about sums him up," Sell acknowledged. "I wouldn't be surprised if the troubles that Burke and his daughter have been having are as much Rumfit's fault as anybody's. You can bet there's a heap more to his breaking with the cattle company than appears on the surface. I dare swear it isn't altogether conscience or skin saving either. There'd be loss of position or money in it somewhere. Maybe both."

"You've more reason to know than I," Haggard said. "This is your stamping ground. Anyhow, the guy's clearly sharp and wary. Last night an attack was made on the Broken B ranch house with dynamite. That's kind of blatant, Sheriff, and could've helped make up his mind to get out." He scratched his chin. "Well, Rumfit's not going to run away now. He'll have to lie up for a while. That should give you every opportunity to pump him."

"He won't talk," the sheriff said. "Especially not if there's a risk of incriminating himself. He's never going to let on that, as range manager for Hamilton Chine, he was in the best position to make life difficult for Tom Burke and Sally. It's been plain to me for a long time that the cattle company wants Sally and her father off their land, but how are you to prove it? So much of it has been made to look like natural disaster, and the actual geography of the business contradicts all the rest."

"That is the killer of it," Haggard admitted. "Yet I do have the glimmerings of an idea that might cover all the facts. It came to me first when I was talking to Sally, and I've been toying with it ever since. If there is anything in it, I may be able to obtain some confirmation of it here in Sheffield."

"How's that?"

"I don't want to go into detail yet, Sheriff," Haggard returned. "I'm going out into the town right now to do some asking around the stores. If I should come up with the evidence I'm looking for, I'll come back here and tell you about it. I fancy we'll need to go riding together. Would you object to that?"

"No," the sheriff said. "I — guess I'm yours to command, sir. The county sheriff would give me seven kinds of hell if I didn't co-operate. Are you talking about Rockford Bend again?"

"We'll see," the marshal replied, pleased that the town lawman appeared willing to help him. "All you've got to do is hold yourself ready. Don't bank on anything. I may have got this all wrong. It happens — too often for Judge Bracknell's liking."

"We all have our crosses," Sell chuckled.

"The rate I'm going on," Haggard growled, "I could soon be nailed to mine." He turned away, passing an eye across the clean and well-kept front of Sell's office, with its neatly stacked desk, polished gun racks, wall maps and photographs of national and local heroes, then stepped out of the street door. "See you anon, Sheriff."

Back on the sidewalk, he went to Sally Burke's red horse and patted its neck absently, head slightly bowed as he thought out what he was going to do — which wasn't all that much in itself — and then he straightened his head and walked off down the street, stopping abruptly at the end of his first thirty paces and staring in what was frankly little short of open-mouthed amazement at the shining elegance of the brougham halted outside Mason's Emporium and the equally scintillating refinements of its female occupant.

The woman, straight of back and poised, had glossy black ringlets of hair fanning across her shoulders, her nose was carefully powdered, and her almond eyes were made up like those of an Egyptian queen. She wore a dove grey suit that fitted her exactly, a lilac silk blouse with a cameo brooch on its front, and a pale purple fedora which came with a gossamer veil. About her neck hung a necklace of pearls, while a Japanese parasol lay open upon the seat opposite her cotton-gloved hands, for it would have been a pretence to suggest that her honeyed complexion needed protection from the Texas sun this early in the day.

Haggard gazed harder and harder at the woman, who was looking away from him and undoubtedly preoccupied. Was it? Could it possibly be? He must have got it wrong! Yet he had never been deceived by a face. And there had been that remark of Chris Daggart's too. The one which had had it, if a trifle cryptically, that Daggart had seen Black Jo Callard in Sheffield. Indeed, the very remark which had brought the marshal here in the first place. Well, if that wasn't Black Jo, Haggard would be damned! Black Jo in the kind of setting which he had felt instinctively to be right for her. The lady — dressed to the part, beautified to the part, and gathered to play the part even now. For she suddenly picked up and closed her parasol, struck its tip audibly upon the floor of the carriage between her feet, and spoke a crisp word to her liveried driver, who moved the brougham on a few yards along the sidewalk and halted again where a big, fleshy man, dressed in a homburg and the finest of black broadcloth, had just stepped out of a shop doorway, a Malacca cane in hand and a diamond stickpin glistening in the front of his full cravat.

The big man just stood there on the boards, nose turned up and expression haughty to a degree, while the woman maintained a similar pose, only seated still, and the driver was forced to climb down from his seat and open the carriage door for the man, who could have performed the act for himself at a minimum loss of energy and none of dignity. Thus he stepped into the brougham, pride and power personified, and seated himself with all the arrogance of some Eastern potentate; while the woman, as if she wished to assess the impression that his lordly behaviour had made upon the simple souls around her, now turned her head to the right and looked across the street.

Her stare clashed instantly with Haggard's. The marshal kept both his gaze and expression rigid. But the woman, taken completely off guard, caught her breath visibly and threw a hand to her throat, the parasol clattering down out of her grasp. Yet, for all her shock, she recovered so quickly that her involuntary behaviour of the second before might not actually have happened, and she adjusted her gaze and looked straight through Haggard — pretending that he was no longer there, if indeed she had ever seen him at all — then bent forward and picked up her parasol, while a word from the man set the carriage rolling for the second time.

Glancing suddenly over the point of his left shoulder, Haggard saw a loafer outside one of the town bars nearby gazing indifferently after the slowly retreating vehicle. "Who would those grand folk be?" the marshal asked, fairly sure that he already knew.

The loafer spat, expressive of what was difficult to tell, then grinned suggestively and said: "That's Hamilton Chine, boss of the cattle company, and the lady is his missus. That Carmilla sure is a sight for sore eyes, hey?"

"Yeah, you can say that again!" Haggard agreed, nodding as he picked up his stride again and moved on. So, he'd got it right — as he had been almost certain he must have — but, in the limited social hierarchy of a primitive community like Sheffield's, that was no great tribute to his powers of discernment. The only thing which had come out of the incident that did matter was his certainty that Carmilla Chine and Black Jo Callard were one and the same. Yet, on all counts, the discovery seemed so preposterous that he didn't know what to do with it. He couldn't just walk up to the woman, waving a Colt forty-five, and tell her straight out who she was. There'd be hell to pay if he did that. It was something he would have to actually prove — and right up to the hilt! Where the hell did you start in on a thing like that? To catch Carmilla Chine while in her guise of Black Jo would be one matter, but to try taking her the other way round would be quite another. In fact it would probably bring a storm of huge dimensions about his ears. That woman was plainly somebody around here, and his knowledge of people warned him that she must hold everybody so much in awe of her that they wouldn't listen to a word he uttered against her. It was a sickener! It never should be! Talk about the devil looking after his own! But, God-dammit, there it was!

The marshal slapped his leg in frustration. This was going to need a heap of thought, and he simply couldn't give his mind to it right now. Yet, secretly — way down where it mattered — he felt a certain relief. Sally's poor dead mother had got it right about him. He did have a liking for the wrong kind of women. And he couldn't deny to himself what was wrong here any more. He loved that blasted female! On no kind of acquaintance at all — he loved her;

and the thought of taking her in, to a life sentence in prison or the possibility of hanging her on the Clarion Town gallows, was almost more than he could bear. It seemed Frank Haggard had gone soft. Or was this heaven's way of punishing him for being the kind of ruthless bastard he had always been when dealing with the wicked? Maybe the avenging angel was just another little imp that the law had borrowed from hell's doorstep. That one would suit the judge all right!

Haggard arrived at the town limits. Here he faced round and looked back down the length of the main street. The first shop nearby that might give a 'yes' answer to the all-important question which he intended to ask was Reagan's Hardware.

Pulling himself together, the marshal crossed over to the sidewalk opposite and entered the Reagan store, where he smiled at the assistant who greeted him and asked: "Do you sell dynamite here?"

"Yes, sir," came the response.

"Have you sold any large amounts of it lately?"

"No, sir."

"How about to the cattle company?"

"They're not among our customers."

"I see."

"Will there be anything else, sir?"

The marshal shook his head, then changed his mind. "Hold on."

"Sir?"

"Where in town does the cattle company deal?"

The assistant threw up his hands in something very like horror. "I can't tell you that. Absolutely not!"

Haggard tapped his badge, but wouldn't press it. He realized that he must have asked one of those questions that in the trade should never be asked; so, feeling a bit of a fool, he left Reagan's and walked on up the main street, coming next to Jethro Plugg's General Store. Here he asked the same vital question concerning the dynamite as he had asked before; and got a similar kind of negative answer. Plugg's store had only a limited sale for high explosives. Folk didn't do a lot of blasting in these parts. There were no mines, few roots big enough to need blowing out of the earth, and no grading or construction work in progress.

Shrugging, the marshal withdrew from Plugg's. A man simply had to persist. He carried on up the street, and arrived next at the gunsmith's shop. Here he was informed that this establishment had never sold high explosives. The gunsmith was interested only in weapons and ammunition. Haggard said that made a lot of sense, then walked on to Bryce and Bryce, Ranch Chandlers, where a garrulous clerk, with a spotty face and a pencil behind his ear, informed him that the chandlers kept plenty of dynamite in stock and could get any amount more within a week. Yes, they had in fact sold a great deal of the high explosive to the Hamilton Chine Company just lately.

Feeling that he had hit the jackpot, Haggard lounged on the counter and requested that the clerk define the words 'a great deal', and the other — perhaps less of a fool than he looked — at once grew wary. He obviously realized that he had let his tongue run away with him and tried to dissimulate and dry up. But Haggard looked stern and tapped on his badge, the request now hanging as a demand between them. "Better part of a ton, Marshal."

"A ton!" Haggard exclaimed. "That's enough to blow up half Texas!"

"Yes, Marshal. But they ask, and we sell."

"What do they aim to do with all that?"

"Dunno, Marshal," the clerk said unhappily. "You'll have to ask them."

"You sure you don't know?"

"Cross my heart and hope to die!"

An older face, seamed and flint-eyed, peered out of a doorway in the wall behind the counter. "He just works here, damn you!"

Haggard tightened up. It wasn't so much the interruption as the manner of it that touched off his anger. "I'm a deputy U.S. marshal," he warned. "If you can't show me any respect, at least keep it polite."

"Then quit chivvying our clerk!"

There was no sense letting this get out of hand. Haggard supposed he could have been slightly at fault. Anyway, he could hear vaguely threatening talk and movement somewhere in the background. A quarrel bordering on the absurd he could do without in here. "I've finished," he said curtly, and began heading back for the street. He had, after all, found out what he wished to know.

Once more in the open air, Haggard found that he had become a trifle disorientated. He needed to relocate the position of the law office, and was surprised to discover that he had walked many yards beyond the building during his progress up the street. Well, as he had walked up the street, so he could walk back down it. And that was what he started to do, only to halt again in a state of dawning amazement as he saw the admirable Carmilla Chine moving towards him on foot, her expression purposeful and fixed. He drew breath to begin speaking but, at the last instant, the woman suddenly averted her eyes and turned to her left down the most unlikely of alleys. More bemused than ever, Haggard watched her shape receding in the direction of the lots. "Jo!" he called after her in what amounted to a theatrical whisper, remembering how he had done something of the same in the evening gloom of the riverside. "Jo!" But again she didn't deign to hear him, and he knew that the old saying about there being none so deaf as those who didn't want to hear remained entirely true.

Again he walked forward, gnawing at his lower lip as he tried to make a little sense of the events in his life at this time, but the seeming confusion and unreality of the day so far went on clinging to his mind, and he was almost startled out of his wits when a shot banged nearby and another followed it like a roaring echo, the bullet slamming into the street and raising a puff of dust about ten feet short of him. Involuntarily going to the draw, he had made a half pull, when a bulky male figure came lurching out of an alley on his right and perhaps seven paces ahead. The other measured his length across the sidewalk, and a smoking revolver spilled slowly from his opening fingers.

Shoving his Colt back fully into leather and putting weight on it through the heel of his hand, Haggard strode up to the prostrate man and bent over him, seeing at once that the fellow was dead, for he had been shot neatly through the back of the skull and brained. Putting a toe under the corpse — since he had already identified who lay there — Haggard heaved the body onto its back and stood looking down into Dan Ward's wide open but empty eyes. He kicked the dead man's gun clear of the fingers which had held it as a matter of course, and then stood back and contemplated the narrow view of the lots that extended beyond the further end of the alley on his right. Nothing moved down there — and he was quite confident that, run as he might, he would find no trace of Ward's killer on the land at the back of the main street — but there was movement closer to hand, and Sheriff John Sell came breasting up to him, an expression of horror and disgust gradually firming on his handsome features. "What the hell are you, Haggard?" he croaked. "The angel of death or something? Men seem to fall around you as if there were a scythe at work!"

"I didn't kill him," the marshal said.

"Then who did?"

"My worst enemy perhaps," Haggard answered soberly. "You tell me, Sheriff."

But Sell didn't even try.

9

IT was the work of a few minutes only to get Dan Ward's body off the street. John Sell, with Haggard staying in the background, asked a number of questions among the bystanders, as his duty demanded — then went off on an inspection of the lots — but he returned to the main, as the marshal had known he would, even more mystified by the shooting than when he had started out. "What do you say to me, Haggard?" he finally asked.

"I told you his name," the marshal said, glancing towards the funeral parlour, whence the dead man's body had been taken. "Dan Ward. He was another member of Black Jo Callard's gang. Dan and I had had words before, Sheriff — not to overstate it — and there's no doubt in my mind that the murderous hellion was about to drygulch me when a friendly gun intervened. That's about the beginning and the end of it, Mr Sell."

"Friendly gun?" the sheriff inquired narrowly. "You mentioned your worst enemy."

"Somebody did it, that's for sure," Haggard reflected. "Figure of speech, Sell."

"I'm not sure I believe you."

"Sheriff, it seems to me one of those days when nobody believes anybody else," Haggard said mildly. "Sure, it's all a great worry to you. Being a lawman is nothing but torment of spirit. It's mostly a fog. You don't know — and I don't know — and neither does the cow, eh?" Though beautifully off-hand, it was of course, as John Sell had suspected, all a long way from the truth; but the marshal didn't feel able to mention the things he knew about Carmilla Chine in any context whatsoever. He was going to keep her out of it for now. Perhaps he owed her — and perhaps he didn't. It was hard to evaluate her guilt, and probably wouldn't get any easier. It must work itself out. These things always did if you gave them time. "Your worry-gutting over Dan Ward won't do any good. You can come back to him later, boy. We've some riding to do. You want to earn your pay, don't you?"

"What have you found out?"

"That's what we've still to find out."

"Don't be a smart ass, Haggard. It doesn't suit you."

The marshal inclined his head in acknowledgement of the fault. "I've learned that the cattle company has recently purchased about a ton of dynamite from Bryce and Bryce. Assuming Black Jo's gang are working for Hamilton Chine just now, it could be that Dan Ward was in the chandlery and heard my inquiries. Perhaps — and I stress the doubt — that was why he was skulking in that alley to blow me sideways."

"That's what I mean," Sell said unhappily. "Suddenly you come out with that gem. Hell's bells, Haggard! Dan Ward may not have been a favourite of yours, but he has the right to process of law. He was murdered."

"He's got the right to six feet of earth," the marshal gritted. "Grow up, John Sell; get the goldurn stars out of your eyes!"

"Grow up to what?" Sell wondered sardonically. "If you're any example — "

"I am," Haggard said flatly, "and a good one. You can always go back to punching cows."

"You seem to hear a lot."

"Because I listen."

"A ton of dynamite, Marshal?" Sell queried. "I don't believe it. Those clowns in the chandlery were pulling your leg! What could the cattle company possibly want a ton of dynamite for? Why you could blow up the whole of this town with that lot!"

"Or change the course of a river maybe?"

"Good God!" the sheriff exclaimed, his face opening like that of one who had just received a vision from above. "Of course! How could I have been so blind?"

"Thought of something?"

"It's obvious now."

"Then tell me about it," Haggard urged, taking Sell by the arm and walking with him to the nearby law office, where they halted on the step and bowed their heads towards each other thoughtfully.

"Many years ago," Sell said, after collecting himself — "long before the Civil War in fact — when my grandfather was a leading light in the local hide-and-tallow trade, a big landslide altered the course of the Pecos at Rockford Bend. The water turned out to the west and made a new channel for itself, coming this way. Before that it bent in the opposite direction and — "

"Flowed through all that dry range the cattle company bought recently," the marshal went on, as his companion paused. "Hamilton Chine means to turn back the clock and make the river go the other way again. It's plain now that Chine wanted Burke and Sally off their land because they were the only people locally who were going to be ruined by his high-handed action. He could've got a hard time in court from them."

"Might still," the sheriff reflected significantly.

"Tom Burke has plenty to tackle the cattle company with. Now we know as much as we know, Chine would be crazy to make further murder attempts."

"That's incidental, Sheriff," Haggard said dismissively. "What's wholly to the point is that we can't let it happen. Forget the rest."

"But can we stop it?" Sell demanded. "I'm talking about using force. I'm talking about plain legally. Say what you like, Marshal, Hamilton Chine owns Rockford Bend, and possession is nine points of the law."

"There's far more to it than that, boy," Haggard said. "The river is a national resource. Chine doesn't actually own any part of the Pecos. The river, from its headwaters to the Gulf, is the property of the State. All business concerning it is the responsibility of the Forest and Rivers division of the Land Department."

"You seem to know a lot about it, Marshal."

"A little anyhow," Haggard replied. "There have been plenty of troubles like this before in Texas. They call this the land of rivers, Sheriff."

"I have to be ruled by you."

"It's all my responsibility," Haggard agreed. "Though how we're to manage this, I probably don't know any more than you do. I guess we'll just have to put it together as we go along — and hope to heck that we don't get our ears shot off along the way."

"That's not my favourite line of talk, Marshal."

"There's a sight too much talk," Haggard admitted. "We're the labourers in the vineyard. Where do you keep your horse?"

"Round the back — in the office stable."

"Fetch it."

Sell gave his head a jerk and turned away, re-entering the law office through its street door. Haggard listened as the sound of the giant's tread receded through the building and ended in the slamming of a rear door and subsequent silence. The sheriff was absent from the scene for about five minutes, then reappeared from the alley at the western end of the office, his right hand at the mouth of a big grey gelding. "Ready when you are," he said.

Haggard untied Sally Burke's red horse from the hitching rail. He stepped up, looking to Sell for guidance. The sheriff, who was also on the street and mounted by now, drew his grey's head westwards and the two lawmen rode carefully along the main — where ranch vehicles were fairly numerous by this hour and the day's trading in full swing — and they trotted over the town's limits and then swung off to the right, hitting up a bit of pace now and heading a little east of north, the path of the Pecos visible out to their right.

Higher ground appeared up front — naked stone breaking back into raw towers and ridges that cut dark lines into the violet skies of the sunless north. "Rockford Bend," the sheriff announced, pointing. "There's plenty of dirt under those bluffs, Haggard, but it would certainly need a hell of a bang to start it slipping again."

The marshal lifted an eyebrow. If he had got it right, 'a hell of a bang' was precisely what Hamilton Chine had in mind for the Bend; but he let it pass, knowing that here again words were being spoken mainly for the sake of it, and they persisted in their ride across the plain that was not without its patches of red baldness, tufts of ant-riddled bunchgrass, and clumps of barrel cacti.

Making no effort to hide themselves, the two lawmen drifted towards the river. Here the land ahead tilted upwards and fell abruptly at them, the waters below the rim settling with slow force into a valley that had obviously — when lined up with the information that John Sell had recently supplied — been at one time a dry cutting and only become a riverbed as the result of that landslip many years ago. From here, by lifting himself in his stirrups and peering along the canted earth below the cañon's rim — into a deep notch that provided a good view of the waters bubbling round from the steep blockage on the other side of the river, where the course itself had been clearly altered by the local cataclysm of maybe forty years ago — the marshal found that he could look right into what he took to be Rockford Bend itself, which was no big feature as these things went and merely the result of ten million years of storm waters from the mountains wearing away at the soft sandstone core of the granite outcrops here and gradually producing the moderately spectacular cutting that was to be the site of the law's present investigation. At this remove, there appeared to be nothing amiss, but Haggard smothered his doubts, recalling what Eli Rumfit had told him about the place — though he could see that they were going to have to cross the river in order to approach its old course — and he suddenly heard himself say to John Sell rather reproachfully: "Shouldn't you have taken us across the Pecos at the town ford, then steered us towards this spot up the opposite bank?"

"You're all right," the sheriff returned shortly. "There's a path below the crags ahead, and a ford no great distance upstream when we hit the lower level again. I came this way because I didn't want it otherwise, did you?"

"Hardly," Haggard growled. "Not that I see anybody on the go around here."

"It all seems pretty dead," Sell admitted. "The better for us — perhaps."

"Cut off the perhaps," the marshal responded. "I've had all the rough stuff I want for one day."

"I wouldn't want more in a year," the sheriff confided.

"A guy your size!" Haggard chipped. "Miss Sally Burke would never believe it!"

"Well, now," Sell said dryly. "We mustn't disappoint Miss Sally, must we?"

"She's all yours, son," Haggard assured him. "Old Tom could do with you around the place."

"You're a knowing devil," the sheriff remarked sourly.

"It goes with the job," Haggard sighed. "You should see that girl's face light up when she speaks of Sheriff John Sell."

"Does that go with the job too?"

"Yours, sure," the marshal acknowledged.

"Get out of here!" Sell snorted, showing a trace more humour than Haggard had supposed he possessed up to then.

Chuckling still, they left the slope under the cañon rim by a neck of soil that was little more than wide enough for a horse to travel safely. After that the two lawmen moved onto the track, mentioned by Sell, which passed beneath the summit crags. The ride was tricky for a minute or two, but not particularly dangerous, and they negotiated the few treacherous spots there were without a bad moment between them. Then, leaving the highest stretch of the path, they started downwards again — a cliff hurtling riverwards on their right — and the way sank quickly enough back to the flat. Here, relaxing visibly, they rode the bank of the Pecos for about a quarter of a mile and then came to a ford — a huge, flat-topped reef of granite in fact that thrust upwards from the bed of the river to within an inch or two of the surface — and crossed over to the eastern shore, after which they followed the walls of another big rock formation round to the dry and thickly grassed channel in which the Pecos had once flowed.

Drawing rein beside a pile of rocks, Haggard swung down and kicked the stiffness out of his legs. After that he looked down into the old watercourse, then lifted his eyes and traced it out into the dusty prairie beyond, judging that the hollow snaked for all of three miles into the country yonder before curving slowly back towards the course which the Pecos followed today. Altogether, the sight was such that it made the marshal amend one or two of his earlier ideas, and he finally turned to John Sell — who had by this time also dismounted and joined him — and said: "That's the better way for the water to go, Sheriff, and I can't deny it. Properly watered, I see thousands of acres of first class grazing over there. But it can't be. No cattleman has the right to take what amounts to an arbitrary decision to beggar others. Broadly speaking, Hamilton Chine could greatly benefit the meat markets by what we believe he's planning, but we know that in truth he's only out to enrich himself."

"Right and wrong," the sheriff commented glumly. "It's a maze Haggard."

"We can only do our best in it," the marshal reminded, running down the side of the old watercourse, checking at the bottom, turning right, and then heading for the huge blockage which had changed the direction of the river's flow, where he could see numerous large excavations in the face of the rearing mass of earth and stone that blocked in the present line of the Pecos.

Walking up to the lowest placed of the excavations — which was situated at the very bottom of the massive dam-up itself — Haggard knelt and studied it, spotting the many grey painted boxes of dynamite which had been thinly buried there, and he glanced round and beckoned for the sheriff to come down to him. "What can't speak can't lie," he remarked, when the other joined him. "From what I can see about it, this blockage is mined from top to bottom, Sheriff. The cattle company intends to blast through it all right."

"Even with all that dynamite present," Sell reflected, passing a shrewd eye over the set up, "I'm not sure it would work."

"All you need's a start," Haggard pointed out. "The weight of the turning river originally brought it this way. Rely on it, those people know what they're doing. They'll have an expert supervising the job."

"So we know the job's on," Sell observed. "Do we ride across to Chine's headquarters and tackle him with what we've discovered at the Bend?"

"I don't see any other way of doing

it," Haggard said. "I'm just surprised, in view of all this dynamite placed here, there's nobody about on guard."

"Does make you wonder a bit," Sell agreed.

By tacit consent, they turned away from the great wall of debris that towered above them and returned to the spot where Haggard had descended the side of the watercourse a few minutes before. They scrambled back to the top of the steeply inclined and tussocky bank with some effort rejoining their horses at once. Again by unspoken agreement, they began leading their mounts back around the red and black-coloured masses of stone that heaved into spires and ridges on their left, and were about to make their final turn towards the ford by which they had recently crossed the Pecos, when a group of men holding guns surged out of some nearby rock-piles and spread across their paths, the muzzles of their rifles and pistols threatening.

Raising his hands high, Haggard came to a stop. He spoke a sharp word, urging his companion to follow his example. John Sell halted to order, but let his right hand drop towards his holster. That was sufficient, and somebody on the other side triggered promptly. The sheriff lurched backwards, blood appearing over his left temple, then slipped to the ground and lay motionless.

Turning towards the fallen Sell, the marshal made to kneel beside him, but the handsome outlaw Chris Daggart, who appeared to be in charge here, barked at him: "You do that, lawman, and you get the same!"

"You'll hang for this one, Daggart!" Haggard promised, fairly seething as he showed the badman his teeth — though still sufficiently even-minded to note that all the men present, with the exceptions of Daggart, Toms, and Dilks — members of Black Jo Callard's gang — were strangers to him and no doubt cattle company employees. "I'll send you through the trap myself!"

"Why can't you keep your long snout out of things, Haggard, blast your eyes!" Daggart raved in response. "If I'd had the sheer luck to live through what you've lived through this last day or two, I'd have gone right straight back home and turned in my badge!"

"But you're not me," Haggard said contemptuously, "and never will be."

The burly, beetle-browed Toms advanced on the marshal, charging him unnecessarily with a lowered shoulder as he appropriated Haggard's revolver. He tossed the weapon to Dilks, whose shoulder-wound, received during the gang's riverside gun battle with the Federal lawman early that day, had still to be cleaned up and bandaged, then crouched beside the town sheriff and examined his wound. "Pah!" Toms announced. "Skull like an old mossyhorn, Chris! That bullet of mine just skidded off the bone! The hellion will come round again, sure as shootin'!"

"If he's lucky," Daggart said stonily. "It all depends on Mr Chine. His word goes."

As if the mention of his name were the necessary spell to perform the magic, Hamilton Chine appeared from the rock-heaps which had previously concealed the men who had stepped out to challenge the two lawmen. Chine moved slowly towards Haggard, tense of feature and peculiarly hunched in his sartorial splendour, as evil-looking, indeed, as any of the other men present on his side. "Marshal," he said, "I've heard a lot about you during the last day or so, and what I've heard I don't like."

"Too bad," Haggard said shortly. "It's as much what I've seen as heard about you that turns me off. You try to look and behave like somebody special, but you're just another fat-bellied cattle baron in fact."

"As Daggart said," Chine warned in the semi-controlled voice of a prideful man boiling inwardly, "I am the power here. You should not provoke me too far."

"If you've got the sense you were born with," Haggard persisted, "you'll fish all that dynamite out of yonder landslip and leave the established shape of the river alone."

"We have been watching for you, Marshal," Chine said. "I deliberately let you have a look at what lies ready to go off. It was obvious that Eli Rumfit had told you all about it."

"What you plan is illegal — and you know it very well!" Haggard stressed. "You wouldn't have tried to murder Rumfit otherwise."

Chine gave a superior smile. "I merely fired him for a series of executive failures."

"Dandy language!"

Now Hamilton Chine made an expansive gesture with his right arm. "Then forget the words. Let's examine the material fact of it. I — or the company of which I am the president — own all the land for miles about us. I — or we — have the legal right to order things on this ground as best suits our ranching operation. No court in the land would quarrel with that."

"But you don't own the Pecos," Haggard retorted. "It's a national resource, and the responsibility of the Land Department in Washington D.C. You can't go altering the course of a major river without their say-so first."

"Not altering the course, Marshal," Chine corrected. "Restoring the river — here — to its original course. You're clearly not a complete fool. You must have seen all that graze to the east of Rockford Bend. The restoration of water to that area will turn it into prime cattle range. Everybody benefits from that."

"Can't deny it," Haggard said. "But that reasoning changes nothing. I guess we have to invoke a sort of custom and practice. What you plan would ruin the Broken B — and, for what I know, a lot of businesses in town that depend on a regular and plentiful water supply.

An act of God changed the course of the river, Mr Chine, and that's mighty different from the act of Man by which you propose to change it back."

"You pathetic ten-for-a-dollar range lawyer!" Chine scorned. "I will not be told by your illiterate like what I can or cannot do!"

"What's happened to the company?" Haggard mocked. "I have to figure the 'we' is about to become a royal one. Sit down with your board, mister, and scratch out a letter to Washington. If the Land Department give you written permission to blast on the other side of this rock, I'll be bound to say no more about it — and we'll just stick to talking about a few smaller matters into which you appear to have thrust a bloody hand."

"I've listened to you," Chine said. "Yes, as much for my own amusement as anything else. But I've heard you out, and not one word of yours has influenced me in the slightest. The Hamilton Chine Company will do as it sees fit within its own boundaries."

"Hamilton Chine has spoken," Haggard said disdainfully. "Big Chief Roaring Wind himself has been heard!"

Chine was mightily affronted, as Haggard had intended, and he passed a reptilian eye from the top of the marshal's head to the tips of his toes and back again. "We are too big to have to worry about little people like you. Little people like those in Sheffield — like those on the Broken B. What voice has the average man, Marshal? Who gives a toss about his misfortunes? Done is done, when power and money strike, and my company has power and money. The local authorities will accept whatever happens here, and Washington D.C. is a very long way off."

"No," Haggard contradicted, touching his breastbone with a fingertip. "It's here — in me. Enough of it to take care of your crimes anyhow."

"Ah, but you are about to become history, Marshal," Chine said malevolently.

"You, sir, are about to vanish from the face of the earth. Before long men will doubt that you ever lived. Not a trace will remain of your life — or John Sell's."

"A riding marshal is never allowed to disappear without trace," Haggard warned. "I have bosses and colleagues who'll leave no stone unturned to find out what became of me. My path is well marked this far. I've been seen by many, and spoken with a few. Can you wipe that out? I'd say it's well nigh indelible!"

"Whatever the law's ultimate finding may be," Chine reminded, "it's almost impossible to prove murder unless a body can be produced. Yours is going to lie under six feet of earth, and above your grave thirty feet of water will flow for evermore." His smile sank into his jowls until it resembled that of an old maneating tiger. "Indeed, Marshal Haggard, you will soon be shot and then buried under what will shortly be the bed of the newly diverted

Pecos river. Possibly some may suspect, yes, but I don't imagine anybody will attempt to see you there, do you?"

Haggard slowly shook his head. He was afraid that Chine had the best of him in that.

10

HAGGARD was ordered to face about, and Chris Daggart stepped up and jammed the muzzle of his sixgun against the lawman's backbone. After that John Sell was picked up and the command given to march. Haggard did so, following the nearby walls of stone as before; then, at the further side of the eastern crags, he allowed himself to be steered into a hidden bay under a dark rockface where a shed of clapboard had been erected and a picket line extended. A good number of horses were tied to the rope, and the marshal stood eyeing these in a vaguely speculative manner while Hamilton Chine moved to the fore and unlocked the shed, revealing that it contained the tools and other equipment which had obviously been used in making the preparations to blast through the huge wall of debris that blocked off the waters of the Pecos from the dry eastern channel nearby.

Entering the shed himself, Hamilton Chine beckoned for Daggart and his friends to follow, the prisoner being brought along naturally in their midst. "Do we tie the marshal up, sir?" Daggart queried fawningly of Chine.

"Most certainly," came the response. "It would be sheer madness to leave him in here unbound!"

"What about the sheriff?" Daggart prompted further.

"Sell, too," Chine replied. "What an embarrassment it would be if he came round in our absence and proved cleverer than he looks."

"Get me some rope, Abel," Daggart said, snapping his fingers at Toms, who was standing with arms akimbo in the doorway.

"Leave the tying up to somebody else, Daggart," Chine commanded. "I need you at work outside. You're my powderman. It was because of your skill with high explosives that I had you brought in at such short notice. There are still plenty of charges to be fused. As I remarked earlier, done is done. Once the Pecos has been diverted into its old channel, it will be virtually impossible to turn the river back again."

"Do my best," Daggart said.

"I require better than that," Chine snapped arrogantly. "You're being paid a small fortune for this work, and I expect you to earn it."

"As to that," Daggart responded, slowly and judiciously, "it's a small fortune for a mighty big job. One mistake — "

"You will make no mistake."

"Reckon not," Daggart agreed, biting at his words. "There are graves to be dug."

"You may decide for yourself who does what work," Chine advised. "Two of your men are still capable of work. Make them dig. Or do you expect me to pay them for nothing?"

"Not me, dammit!" protested Dilks, who had a filthy neckerchief clapped to a wounded shoulder that was still trickling blood. "I've already had a lump shot off me in your service, Mr Chine!"

"You won't die of it!" Chine sniffed heartlessly. "If you hadn't bungled your task, fool, you wouldn't have got hurt. I think you can still dig."

"You'll have to, Oran," Daggart warned. "Abel Toms won't dig alone."

"Hell, dammit, and kick the devil's butt!" Oran Dilks cursed bitterly. "I should've done what Lance Cowper did after he stopped lead. I shoulda pulled out and gone to see the sawbones."

"Too late for all that," Daggart said shortly. "We got ourselves a situation, son. Get today over and you may be able to lay up for a while, eh?"

Dilks spat out a filthy expletive, yellow teeth grinding in his thin, unshaven jaws.

At that moment Abel Toms re-entered the hut. He carried a pair of lariats in his right hand. "Here you are, Chris," he said, holding out the ropes expectantly.

"Get on with the tying yourself!" Chine barked at the stocky, tough-looking outlaw. "It seems to me you men have to be told everything."

"That's on account of how we're trained by guys like you," Toms retorted. "You've just gotta give orders! I ain't one of your lackeys, my fine sir, and don't you treat me so!"

"Get on with it, Abel!" Daggart commanded. "Mr Chine isn't going to take any of your lip!"

"You climb down, Chris," Toms cautioned, his eyes no more than menacing slits and his right hand close to his holster. "You push me one inch more, mister, and I'll get really nasty. We've done our share o' bickering many a time. It'll come to the pull. You know it, and I know it. Might as well be now."

"This is neither the time nor the place," Daggart pleaded. "I've got some tricky work to do. Ease off, man — ease off. Simmer down! Nobody wants to rub you raw. We undertook a job."

"You undertook a job!" Toms corrected. "Black Jo would skin us if she knowed about it!"

"As to that," Daggart sighed, "she most likely does. She may even have put me up for it. All this being a rushed job."

"Chris, I don't get you," Toms said more soberly.

"Likely you will one of these fine days," Daggart said dismissively. "We've got work to do, man. It's our lot. You going to get on with a share of it?"

"Well, are you, Toms?" Chine asked in a far more reasonable tone of voice than he had been employing recently; and he shifted his stance and set up a dull jingling of gold coins in his trouser-pocket.

Toms alerted to the sound, a greedy glint rising from the depths of his murky eyes. "Awright," he growled. "You want them two lawmen tied up?"

"That's it," Daggart agreed. "Take yourself a shovel after that — you and Oran both — and get down into the dry riverbed yonder and dig a good deep grave for two."

"Okay."

Chine jerked his head quickly at Daggart. The businessman's expression seemed to suggest that they should make themselves scarce before any new trouble blew up. The two walked outside together — and vanished about their own affairs — while Dilks held his sixgun on Haggard and kept stirring nervously at the still unconscious town sheriff with a toe. This obviously caused Abel Toms some irritation, for he suddenly turned on Dilks and snarled: "Consarn it, Oran, that big son-of-a-bitch ain't goin' to come to this side o' night! You get clipped by a slug how he did, boy, and it needs a real long sleep to get over it. So just — just stop it, will you?"

"Blast me if you ain't a trial at times, Abel!" Dilks complained.

"Now that's Daggart talk!" Toms warned narrowly. "Aw, them sidewinders get on my wick, Oran! How did we suddenly get mixed up in all this? I was never comfortable around dynamite. My daddy died when a bagful of it went up in a mine on the Comstock."

"Ain't that too bad!" Dilks observed rather callously. "Hadn't you better look sharp about hogtyin' that marshal? We got diggin' to do. That takes time."

Toms cast a noose over Haggard's head and shoulders, pinning the marshal's arms as he drew it tight. Then, after passing several more turns of the rope about the lawman's body, he kicked Haggard's legs from under him and completed a body-length binding with all the skill of an old hand. During the next minute or two, Toms did much the same for the senseless John Sell; and after that, showing a great deal more energy than before, he picked out a shovel from a line of tools propped against the wall on his right and passed it to Dilks, who had just holstered his now redundant Colt and was flexing what amounted to his one good hand. Finally, having selected a double-jack for himself, Toms led Dilks to the door and they went out, the stocky badman's face coming round in an evil grin as he made to close up the shed behind them. "Next time we come in, Marshal," he jeered, "I reckon you'll be dead. Likely that fat skunk, Hammy Chine, will have blown your brains out for himself. If he ain't done it, Marshal, I've got a gun. Savvy?"

"Get out of here, stinkpot!" Haggard rasped.

The door shut and the latch fell. Haggard heard the two outlaws walking out of the hidden bay. They were laughing between themselves and dragging their iron digging tools across the rock floor of the place. The metallic scraping noise thus produced set the nerves on edge, but this sound — like that of the retreating footfalls — soon faded out, and the marshal found himself left in a state of silence which tested his mettle as much as anything that had gone before.

Haggard let his aching head rest against the naked stone of the shed's floor. The sensations in his body as a whole were indescribably unpleasant. His existence just lately seemed to have contained one crisis after another. He was a better man than most, and knew it, but there was a limit to what the fibre of even the toughest could take, and he was near to it. Yes, there had been seeming miracles in his life, past and present, but now he needed another one. He was afraid that no man could walk fortune's knife-edge as he had so often done and not take an eventual fall. Perhaps today was the day on which his luck was destined to finally run out. If so, he must prepare himself to face the end with what equanimity he could muster. There was no consolation. He had done his duty, yes — and there were colleagues as hard and dedicated as he who might remember him with respect — but it was a cold outlook, and he asked himself whether, in terms of normal life, he had ever lived at all. The answer that he heard in his head was an echoing 'no', and he felt totally despondent. Yet, he supposed, as he viewed all the things he had not had: home, women, children, education, leisure — that nobody could have it all. There had to be regrets at the end of every life. While a man should feel fulfilled in terms of all the things he'd had, it seemed that in fact he could only feel unfulfilled in terms of the things he hadn't had. There was no satisfaction in any of it — no profit under the sun! Perhaps it would be better for him if it were all over.

At a very low ebb, Haggard didn't have a lot of thought for much else just then, and he supposed vaguely that he was listening to the invading presence of a muskrat or something of the kind when he heard movement down in the right-hand corner of the shed's further end. Now, glancing that way — though the angle lay in almost impenetrable shadow — he glimpsed a gently writhing shape which he sensed rather than saw was human. Lifting his upper body to the extent that he could, Haggard peered intently into the corner and realized that the intruder was flattened against the ground as a man could never flatten himself. That athletic spread of the pelvis was uniquely female and had a trace of the serpent about it. Altogether, the marshal felt no doubt that a woman was crawling into the shed at a spot where the exact shaping of its base met a hollow in the exterior rock level which had been left to serve as its floor. The female had to be one of the slimmest and most lithe of kinds to enter through such a narrow gap, and Haggard was quite certain that had he been on the outside and attempted to enter in the same fashion, he would not even have got a start, short of lifting the entire clapboard structure with the back of his neck and shoulders.

The woman's hips set up a final writhing and she raised her upper body off the floor by bracing her arms. It was by sheer strength that she drew herself fully into the shed. After that she gathered herself into a crouch and then sprang to her feet, revealing herself in what light entered the building through the small and dusty window on the lawman's left as Carmilla Chine — though in the garb and guise of Black Jo Callard on this occasion — and, reaching Haggard's bound figure in three light strides, she sank down beside him and fished out a penknife from the breast-pocket of her black silk shirt. Opening the little knife's blade, she quickly examined the bonds that held the lawman fast and then began sawing at them, first severing the round of hemp that was mainly responsible for securing his arms and then the one that did the same job on his legs. Before long, with some further help from the knife and a bit of kicking and struggling on his own part, Haggard found himself free of his bindings and stood up, pleased that he had not lain bound for a sufficient length of time for his limbs to have stiffened to any extent. "What am I to say, Jo?" he asked. "That's twice in one day you've saved my bacon!"

"You're not out of here yet," the woman cautioned.

"Yet you'd have seen me killed to start with," Haggard mused, frowning down at her as he sought understanding. "There's an inconsistency in that. Is it all fondness?"

"You flatter yourself, Marshal!" Black Jo mocked.

"Do I?"

"The first was for the gang."

"And since?"

"For the cattle company," she answered swiftly. "It is more my creation than my husband's."

"I can see how that might be," Haggard admitted, a trifle sobered — since he realized now that his unaccustomed romantic ardour could have been more of the imagination than the brain itself. "So — if that's all of it, why free me? Wouldn't I be better dead in the Chine interests?"

"No," she replied shortly. "My husband is a vain fool. He regards himself as big enough to get away with anything. The company hasn't even the money he pretends to — "

"So that's why you've been running that gang of yours!" Haggard cut in. "You've been riding the back trails to finance your husband up front!"

"He's a good businessman in many respects," Black Jo responded, "but he will overreach himself. The herd he recently bought in Carlsbad is an example of that."

"The one he wants to put on that stretch of waterless grass yonder?"

"I imagined you'd have heard about it," the woman said, nodding. "But the grass isn't waterless. We could dig waterholes over there, but that takes time. Hamilton is in too much of a hurry. He wants it all — now, if not sooner!"

"I think I get you," Haggard said wryly. "I'd seen it for myself, and even taxed your old man with it." He nodded approvingly. "You're a wise woman, Jo. It is madness to brace the Government. If Hamilton Chine is allowed to divert the Pecos just here, he'll upset a lot of people and Washington will have to come into it. He couldn't possibly win. Otherwise — done your way — it's all here for the taking. A little patience and he can have all the wealth he wants. Quite legitimately."

"Exactly," Black Jo agreed. "The murder of a Federal lawman — on cattle company land — would be the ultimate act of madness. One from which Hamilton could never come back."

Haggard laughed softly into his hand. "I thought you loved me, Jo. But here we have the fact of it. A mite of emotional blackmail, eh? I owe you.

Pay up, dog, for services rendered."

"Yes, that's what it amounts to, Marshal."

"If you get me out of this, I'm to hold my row?"

"You're an articulate man," the woman acknowledged brazenly.

Haggard drew a deep breath. "I may not be able to do that. There are people besides myself who are at least partly in the know."

"But you're the one who matters," Black Jo reminded. "Your reports are all that count. You've been out hunting outlaws. You don't have to write — or speak — a word concerning Sheffield and the Hamilton Chine Cattle Company."

"There's truth in that," the marshal admitted. "All manner of crimes have been committed hereabouts, you know, but it could be possible — in that nobody who matters is dead. So far."

"You see?"

"No. I see only what you're seeing." Haggard frowned anew. "All this is ultimately dependent on the river staying as it is. I couldn't do a thing, even in the strictest sense, if that dynamite over there blows. Are you sure, Jo, that you've thought this through as clearly as you ought?"

"Oh, we're wasting time!" she declared tautly. "I had no intention of talking to you like this!"

"I just asked you a question," Haggard reminded her.

"There's — there's too much of it," Black Jo admitted. "I — I can't control it that readily. I'll force Hamilton to forget his plan. Most of the men present will obey me more readily than him!"

"There's the weakness," Haggard said heavily. "You have nothing clear-cut on offer. This is a lash-up, Jo. Something you put together on the spur of the moment."

"It had to be so!" she confessed. "I feared this was going to happen when I saved you in town. It was necessary to get home and change.

I — I hadn't — Oh, we must get moving!"

"It is me you're worried about," he said quietly, yet not without a feeling of triumph. "You'd have done better to keep out of it, wouldn't you?"

"Heaven knows!" Black Jo answered dismally. "Frank, don't waste your chance. They will kill you!"

Haggard stepped towards her. He wasready to take her into his arms — and to blazes with everything else! — when a man outside the door, who seemed to be angrily soliloquising, said: "A plague on Oran Dilks! So he's gotta have a lighter shovel, has he? Well, I'll git him one! Damned if I'm going to do the diggin'!" Then the latch shuddered and Abel Toms came bursting into the shed, his face like the proverbial thundercloud — and his jaw fell as he saw the marshal and Black Jo standing together. "What — what — ?" he gobbled, his eyes starting to pop, and he went instinctively for his gun.

Black Jo did likewise. She had a

silver-plated Smith and Wesson thirty-two calibre pistol on her right hip. It was out almost faster than the eye could follow and spitting fire. Toms dropped his weapon as it cleared leather; then, his eyes bulging in ever greater disbelief, clutched at the middle of his chest and slipped to the floor, where he kicked abruptly onto his back and lay in complete stillness.

"That's done it, Jo!" Haggard gritted, snatching up the dead Toms' fallen Colt. "I've got a fight on my hands! You stay in here! Your husband will protect you!"

"He won't!" Black Jo retorted, her mouth firming resolutely. "He'll see this as betrayal! I'll stick with you!"

"Are you crazy?" Haggard demanded, shaking his head at her in horror.

It was no good. The woman leapt past him and out of the shed. Haggard followed as swiftly as he could. Before them tossed and surged the newly spooked horses at the picket line, while beyond the creatures a pair of cowboys — to whom the marshal could not put names — stood gazing at the shed in startlement. The two men made no attempt to draw their guns, but they did begin to shout at the tops of their voices, and this noise further upset the frightened mounts and caused them to jostle, bump, and rear with such violence now that Haggard saw at once that there was no chance of being able to cut out two of the animals and calm them down in the confined space of the hidden bay for riding purposes. Escape on horseback, from this spot, was plainly out of the question.

"This way!" Black Jo urged, pointing along the side of the shed and into the tiny open area at the further end of the bay from which she had entered the fragile building not so long ago.

Haggard pursued the female, hard put to it to keep up. She seemed to know what she was doing, and he had no ideas of his own. Within moments they reached the limit of the shed.

Then they rounded the end of the building and, still in full flight, sprang onto the lower teeth of a jagged arch of rock which connected the bay with the first ridges of the heights above. Now, obeying the energies that drove them, they climbed frantically, treading a precarious path towards a ledge about sixty feet up that curved out to the left and joined the top of the huge wall of debris which contained the present course of the river Pecos on its western side.

The marshal heard voices calling from positions all over the landslip. He cast a glance round and down, and saw eyes peering up at him and Black Jo. Points of fire began to blink, and shots boomed, the echoes falling back dully as slugs clipped the rock about the two fugitives and sent jagged splinters flying.

Haggard heard Hamilton Chine urging the marksmen on. He tried to go faster, but checked in momentary agony as lead scored the back of his right arm.

Angered, he looked for the source of that ominously accurate shot and saw Chris Daggart aiming at him from high on the slope nearby. The outlaw was in fact not more than twenty yards away, and more or less on the same level as himself. Knowing that he mustn't let the other get off another shot, Haggard cocked the late Abel Toms' revolver and fired across his own body. He scored a bigger success than he might have expected, for Daggart jerked together violently and spun like a top where he stood, pitching down the acclivity after that and finally sliding to the bottom on his back, where he lay spreadeagled, his soles pointing upwards and his arms outflung on the grass behind his head.

Certain that Hamilton Chine was now in need of a new powderman and would not be exploding any dynamite today, Haggard scrambled on to the ridge for which Black Jo had been heading, at the woman's heels. His first instinct was to break right, where

243

buttresses of stone offered protection from the still numerous bullets flying around and a continuation of the ridge itself followed the curve of the brink above the river northwards; but the woman pulled him back and, pointing across the top of the landslip said: "It's a dead end if you follow the ridge round, but if we go this way it will be easy to descend into the grass to the south of Rockford Bend."

"I leave it to you!" Haggard gasped.

But just then Black Jo emitted a sharp cry and fell to her left knee, clutching at her upper body, and it was clear that she had been hit by a bullet and quite badly hurt. Haggard gazed down at her, quivering with shock, then peered across the slope to the east of him, seeking where the bullet had come from, and he spotted Hamilton Chine himself brandishing a sixgun not so many feet below. Taking a minimum of aim, he blazed at Chine — and went on triggering at the businessman until his Colt was empty — and he had the impression that every one of his slugs hit the big man's torso. Chine remained erect for a moment longer, probably dead on his feet, then crumpled into a shapeless heap and lay with smoke from his smothered gun creeping out from beneath his body.

Ashen-faced, Black Jo — or Carmilla Chine — had watched her husband's death without a sound, and now, forcing herself upright with an effort, she said: "Goodbye, Frank." Then she turned and staggered rapidly to the opposite brink, throwing herself off it before Haggard was fully aware of what she intended.

Starting after her too late, the marshal heard a splash from the river far below. Then all was silent, apart from the sporadic banging of a gun in the hand of somebody who had yet to realize that it was all over.

11

HAGGARD teetered on the brink from which Black Jo had jumped a second or two before. He peered downwards, his hurtling gaze attempting to pierce the gloomy waters that swept through the cañon below. All the time he was praying to God that the woman would surface where he could see her, but nowhere did the top of the water break and give him a glimpse of her.

A pulse throbbed dully in the marshal's brain, and a kind of madness filled him. He couldn't let this end so weakly; he could not simply abandon a woman for whom he had such intense feelings. In some strange way Black Jo was hope to him — if that wasn't the greatest folly of it all — and he felt that, living or dead, he'd got to find her, even if that meant passing through hell itself.

Feet-first, he sprang into space. Down he rushed, the air hissing past him, and into the river he plunged, arrowing down to the very floor of the cold depths. Here mud swirled and sand rushed, and sight was more imagination than reality. Finding his buoyancy and catching his submerged balance, Haggard began to swim, crawling around the bottom of the Pecos like a demented crustacean, but of Black Jo Callard there was still no trace.

The need to surface became imperative. Indeed, Haggard found himself close to drowning when he broke through. Treading water, he fought for life — a battle he gradually won — and he let the tumble and swirl of the conflicting currents bear him southwards and out of Rockford Bend, the high walls of the cañon slowly diminishing on either hand until they were no longer there.

Now the prairie grass clothed the

banks on either hand, and he was in the softly bubbling hush of an idyllic dream world. The sun shone down on him brightly out of a clear blue sky, and the surface of the river spread around him in glistening circles of light. He felt the warmth of noon on his face, and the madness of a short while ago slowly drained out of him, leaving his familiar sanity behind it.

Life went on. He responded to the universal maxim. Black Josephine was dead. His common sense told him that it was better so. Her continued existence could have embroiled him in heaven knows what! He would probably have told lies for her, until the sheer weight of the falsehoods destroyed them both. A man could not get away with trying to protect the guilty. Those who transgressed must pay their own bills. Their sins were their own. And, make no mistake about it, even if, in that unspeakable way of his, he had loved the woman, she had been, particularly in the guise of Black Jo Callard, as guilty as any person behind whom the prison doors had ever slammed shut. She hadn't deserved a break. She hadn't deserved a second chance. She hadn't deserved a guy like him. He had been cleansed by the waters of the Pecos. It was time to forget her. If — he could.

The waters ran fleet, and the current carried Haggard towards the river's eastern bank. Presently, with a bed of sand and round flints shifting underfoot, he stood up uncertainly and waded ashore, shaking himself as he entered the reeds and grasses along the water's-edge. Then he checked abruptly, peering at the ground adjacent, for there were broken straws and flattened weeds which suggested that somebody had emerged ahead of him near this spot. No, the signs were old and had probably been made by an animal. There was just the sky, and the empty land, the aching miles, and the illusion of new worlds on the far horizon. If anybody had stepped out of the river around here in the last few minutes, they would still be in full view of him now. "Jo," he muttered to himself. "Jo."

Well, what about it? A year from now — ten years from now. A man never lost the hope that one day he might turn a corner on to something that he had believed gone for ever.

THE END